TheHappyStoryGarden.com

Author, Illustrator and translator - Zinaida Kirko
Editor - Igor Kirko
Translator and Editor - Leslie Harwood
Book creation - Viktoriia Harwood

In the vast reaches of space, on the far edge of Orion's belt, young racer Joe Dee Myers isn't just competing, he's fighting for his planet's survival. His skills behind the wheel are unmatched, but speed alone won't save his dying world. Ruthless rivals, sabotage, and looming conspiracies threaten to crush his world before the finish line.

To defy fate, Joe must push beyond his limits.

Can he secure his planet's future against all odds?

Find out in this thrilling sci-fi adventure for all ages.

TheHappyStoryGarden.com

2025

GO, JOE!

Book 1

Zinaida Kirko

GO, JOE!

Book 1

Zinaida Kirko

Contents

Chapter 1.

The Monster

The engine grunted and coughed like an old man, and it seemed that every breath it took would be its last. But Joe was delighted. He stomped on the pedal, and the racing car, cobbled together from old parts, shuddered and trembled, emitting a fearsome roar. Tossing his light brown curls, Joe laughed.

"Seventh Star! It's a monster! That's what I'll call it - Monster!"

Despite his lame leg, Ike, Joe's mechanic, nearly jumped for joy at Joe's reaction. "I've been fixing it up all week," he said.

Joe spent everything he earned from racing into his inventions, and Ike worked for him alone, not only for the money, but for the passion they shared. At just sixteen, Joe had achieved more success than champions twice his age.

"How long have I got before the race?" Ike looked at his watch.

"Thirty-four minutes."

Joe touched the bracelet on his arm. A screen appeared in front of him displaying the faces of the other racers.

"Ram, Kort, Dewey, Virta... this should be easy," he laughed. "I'll be first for sure."

"Preferably." Ike hesitated. "You owe me a lot...and prices are rising by leaps and bounds. The next Monster will be almost twice as expensive."

But Joe didn't listen. He shoved the stick in gear and pressed the gas pedal with all his might. There was a squeal of rubber, and clouds of dust obscured everything as Joe and his Monster disappeared over the horizon.

Ike's timid assistant mechanic Noi approached him almost on tiptoe. He was terribly thin and half the size of any human, due to his alien origin, a fact that almost no one knew. Joe gave him a feeling of irrational fear, so he avoided the racer as much as he could. But, when he was not there, Noi would talk about nothing else other than how he tightened the nuts in Joe's cars. He craned his neck, peering into the clouds of dust.

"Do you think he will win this time, too?"

"I bet everything on him." Ike balanced his lame leg against his crutch. "I hope this will cover at least part of the debt. One way or another, he loses only when he does not participate."

Noi shook his head in fear, as if Joe would appear out of nowhere at any moment.

"Noi thinks he has a great future...great!" "He has no future." Ike smirked.

Noi's eyes widened, ready to pop out of their sockets.

"They say he saves up all the winnings to leave the planet."

"He's not going anywhere! He gives all the winnings to me. Don't get me wrong, I love him like a son, but I've known him since childhood. He is a half-wit, you know, and on top of that, he considers himself one of the Gurts and is proud of it."

The Gurts were the lowest class on the planet Melgera. They hardly ever studied or worked, huddled in little dirty houses in the worst quarters, and did whatever they wanted. But they had a philosophy that they were proud of; they simply despised all rules and order. They called it freedom.

Ike pulled out a flask and took a sip, then screwed up his face. "Oh my, there's only dust! No water left on this planet!"

"Take mine," Noi handed him a small bag.

"I'd rather die than drink this mud." Ike spat out everything that was in his mouth. "Come on, we'll be late for the race."

Limping, he moved to the exit, and Noi continued to peer at the horizon until the clouds of dust disappeared and the view of the desert steppe became clear.

◉ ◉

Chapter 2
The Monthly Race

The Star stadium, with an open area and a racing track, was full of Gurts who stood, sat, and even hung from the rafters of the makeshift rusty hanger structure.

"Joe! Joe! Joe!" they chanted. "Deee! Deee! Deee! Myyyyyyers!" Again and again.

The rest of the racers wiped their cars with disgruntled faces. They shuddered and turned around when occasionally someone called out their names: Virta, Kort or Dewey. Ram was a newcomer, no one shouted his name or even looked at him.

Virta's face twisted with contempt when the Monster roared out onto the site.

"Stupid Oran. Why is he even allowed here?"

"That's why." Dewey pointed at the roaring crowd.

Orans was the name given to those who belonged to a higher cast. And Joe, we can assume, was one of them, although he had Gurt roots.

He got out of the car, tossed his curls, and looked around at everyone present with his piercing clear blue eyes.

The stadium roared.

"Joooe! Joooe! Joooe!" and again, "Deee! Deee! Deee! Myyyyyyers!!!" Ike approached him with his limp and opened the hood.

"You've worn the car out before the race."

"Come on, I just warmed it up a bit."

Joe smiled his boyish smile, waved to the stadium, and sat back down. Then he pressed the button on the bracelet. Numbers swirled beside his laughing face. Five thousand subscribers! That was one thousand more than in the last race!

But Joe knew he shouldn't be thinking about that. He sighed and touched the bracelet again. A screen appeared in front of him showing several people in plain gray suits. It was a speech by the Ministry of Interplanetary Relations. Joe knew that if he didn't watch it, his mother would be furious, because among the speakers there was one tall, thin person with a particularly dull face - his elder brother Ulit.

It was thanks to Ulit that Joe's family moved from the Gurt to the Oran estate. Ulit studied for a long time and made a career, then became an ambassador in the Ministry of Interplanetary Relations. But because of this, Joe was ashamed. He was proud that he was a Gurt, proud of their freedom, anarchy, and the fact that absolutely everything could be sent to hell. Having him as a brother spoiled it all.

"Melgera's water resources are close to being depleted and funding required for the necessary work can only come from the interstellar committee of Orion, but as you all know, we were not even allowed there..." Ulit mumbled on monotonously.

"Seventh Star, why is it always so boring?"

Joe turned off the screen and took out a jar of oil.

"Is it your brother on the screens again?" Ike was tightening some screws.

"Dull, like this whole planet." Joe shook his curls, moistened a cloth with oil and wiped the tattoo on his arm.

It was a winged bird-lizard with an open mouth - a symbol of the Gurt community.

"Don't worry, soon you will leave this planet, as you dreamed." Ike winked at him. "I don't know how much you saved, but you owe me a lot."

Joe looked at the tattoo. It was shining.

"I promise I'll give you everything I win today."

Ike nodded, but the blaring loudspeaker in the stadium swallowed his response, making it impossible to hear over the booming sound.

"Welcome, welcome, welcome to all those present at our monthly race! And today the prize is twelve thousand Kharts! I hope you all have already placed your bets because in front of you today, ready to break the racing horizon..." and the announcer began listing the names of the drivers. However, they were all drowned in one long chant:

"Jooooe! Jooooe! Jooooe! Deeeee! Deeeee! Deeee! Myyyyyyyers!!!"

Joe went out, greeted everyone, and then pointed his finger at the crowd, nodding his head as if he knew each of them.

He turned to the drivers and his gaze settled on Virta. She whispered something in her sister's ear, looking straight at Joe. Meeting his gaze, she grinned and turned to her car. Her sister giggled and trotted off to the audience platform.

"Five…four…three…"

Joe got into the car, put on his racing goggles, and started the engine.

"Two…ooooone!!!"

The cars took off, raising clouds of dust. Noi ran out of the crowd and onto the road.

"Go, Joe, go!" he shouted.

But the audience was already looking at a screen that appeared in front of them in the air. On it, five racing cars were rushing forward through the hilly desert area; out in front of course, was the Monster.

Chapter 3

The Bad Day

This day was especially hot. Inside the cabin, the air was so stifling, Joe was having difficulty breathing. With one hand he took out a flask, took a sip, and nearly choked on the dust. But he was used to this taste. Since childhood, it seemed pleasant to him, despite the fact that over the years there was more and more dust and less and less water.

Joe looked in the wing mirror. Ram was far behind, but Dewey and Virta were both nearer. "I wonder where Kort is?" he thought. "Whatever. He is definitely behind." The racer stepped on the gas and the engine rumbled loudly in response.

Hills grew to the right, a dry grove to the left. A long time ago, he still remembered, they were green. Ahead, stars were visible in the pink sky. In this part of Melgera, they could be seen even in daylight. Joe seemed to be heading straight towards them.

"Where there is no horizon and the bottom is not seen, the Seventh Star shines, clear and bright, like a dream..." He sang this song whenever he felt stressed. "Why is the star the seventh?" he thought. "Who can count the stars?"

However, he didn't have time to dwell on that much longer as suddenly, Virta appeared in a rusty old banger beside him and hit him with all her might. Joe stepped on the gas and, seizing the moment, hit her back even harder. Yes, her motor was not weak, but she couldn't even imagine what good old Ike enhanced his Monster with. Joe laughed as he looked in the mirror at her trying to turn the stalled car around.

Dewey appeared nearby. Where is he going? Joe knew the racing landscape very well. There are marshlands to the right. It would be a good idea to squeeze him so he had no option but to take the right track,

even if this maneuver would delay him, too. The gamble paid off, and within a few seconds, Dewey flew into the swamp.

Meanwhile, Kort caught up with him, but Joe easily ensured he didn't overtake. Kort's car was almost new, straight from the manufacturer. But these people knew nothing about the mechanics of racing cars. Joe easily kept him behind, simply by pressing the turbo booster as hard as he could.

"Poor Ram," he thought as he drove towards the finish line. "Maybe he won't even make it to fifth place."

But at that moment, something moved fast in front of him. What was it? A small animal ran and stopped right in Joe's path. "A Sand Meerkat?" He pushed the brake and turned the steering wheel.

The car flipped and fell on its side. Joe got out as fast as he could and ran a safe distance. The poor old Monster exploded on the spot and burst into flames. Somewhere in the distance, Virta's sister's face flashed before him just as Kort crossed the finish line.

"Run, Joe, run!" he heard a voice saying. Who's?

It was Noi. He squealed as loudly as he could. And Joe ran as fast as possible. In a few seconds, he reached the finish line, where a ribbon with the number "2" was hung around his neck.

The stadium hummed in frustration. Kort proudly climbed out of the car, waving his hands. But no one celebrated his victory. Everyone was making a loud noise. They were yelling and shouting Joe's name in anger.

Joe looked back, Monster was still ablaze, but no one appeared happy he survived. Even Ike just pursed his lips and slapped him on the shoulder.

"Second place isn't that bad," Joe said apologizing as they entered the locker room.

"Yes," Ike replied, "but do you have any idea how much money they bet on you? How much did I bet on you? And now you've lost the car.."

"But why bet only on me, if...?"

"If you won the last eight times in a row!" he replied.

Everyone knew that coming first again would have equaled Toto Graf's record of winning nine times in a row. Ike was angry and kicked everything in his path. Noi trotted behind them.

Dewey entered the dressing room. He was covered in mud but seemed happy.

"What is it like being number two?"

"Not as bad as being number four," the racer shrugged. Noi laughed as if it was the funniest joke ever.

"Be quiet, you waste of space, or I'll fire you!" Ike shouted at him. "Listen, Ike," Joe said, "if it wasn't for that meerkat…"

"They say sand meerkats are an ancient symbol of Melgera," Noi interrupted.

"Are you some kind of stupid Oran? Or where did you read it?" Ike loomed over Noi so that he sat down.

"Ike, I will return everything." Joe pushed him away from the mechanic.

"In the next race we will win again, and I promise, I will return everything!"

"Everything?" Ike gritted through his teeth. "I bet everything on you today! And lost everything! It's not even about the money." He shook his head. "I thought...we all thought you were...a legend!"

He turned, looked at laughing Dewey with contempt, and left, almost pushing Ram as he went.

Joe sighed, looking back at him.

"And Noi thinks you were at your best," said the alien, stepping back. "There, near the swamp...such a classic maneuver. And you immediately knocked the girl out of the game."

But Joe didn't listen. He left the locker room and rushed towards the house. The groups of Gurts parted, giving him way.

"How could you, Joe? Who paid you to lose? We bet everything on you! Joe, you're a traitor!" some shouted after him.

But it was better than the silent looks of the majority.

Joe walked for a long time. He destroyed the car, and he was unlikely to be able to save up for a new one. Was this really the end of his racing career?

He left the Gurt quarter and went towards the cleaner Upper City of Orans.

It was getting dark outside. He reached the hill and looked down. In the hollow where the clouds were creeping up from the mountains, the lights of the Lower City of the Gurts were burning. That was his home, not here. But, alas, he let them down. He betrayed them all. They would never chant his name again, and now he was in exile.

◉ ◉

Chapter 4
Must Try

Joe came out onto a broad street lined with rich Oran houses. He stopped and looked around, and then, making sure no one could see him, pulled his sleeve down to cover the bird-lizard tattoo. In those moments he hated himself, but such was the price of living in two worlds.

When he reached one of the richest houses in the area, he went towards it and looked through the living room window. His mother, Sheila, was setting the table at which Ulit was sitting. He was telling her

something and gesticulating intensely, which was unusual for him.

As quietly as he could, Joe opened the door and tiptoed into the hallway. If he was careful, he could get past them unnoticed. He took two steps.

"Joe!" came a stern voice from the kitchen.

The racer sighed and turned towards the sound.

The dining room was clean and neat as always. He was immediately reminded that he was covered with dust from head to toe.

"Joe," Sheila softened her voice and invited him to sit down.

Ulit adjusted his glasses and smiled. But the racer collapsed on a chair, crossed his legs, and clicked his tongue. He knew what was about to begin.

"Have you watched Ulit's speech?"

"Of course."

"And you don't want to say anything about it?"

The question took Joe by surprise, and he thought he should have been better prepared. He shrugged, avoiding his mother's gaze.

"Didn't you find it shocking?"

Ulit and Sheila looked at each other and Joe felt their condemnation and judgment and the fact that he, as always, was out of his element.

"Look," he began conciliatorily, "I did watch his speech. And I think I was shocked. But just because it was so boring," he laughed. "It was boring. Nerdy and boring by miles, as always!" He spread his hands and then clapped.

Ulit turned pale.

"The water is practically finished," he said.

"It's always been that way," Joe snapped, "for as long as I can remember! All of you ..." he pointed around with his hand as if there was a crowd, "only aggravate the situation by inflating fears. Gurts don't believe in it. They just don't! It's a myth."

"Gurts?" Sheila threw a plate on the table. "All that we have is also thanks to the Gurts? If not for Ulit, you would have continued to eat dust in their rusty hangars!"

"Don't, please, don't." Ulit tried to calm her down.

"Get out!" Mom said through gritted teeth.

Joe seemed to be waiting for just that. He cheerfully jumped up from his seat and stomped out of the dining room in an exaggerated manner.

When he got to his room on the top floor, he turned on the light and slammed the door. It was a spacious place with a large bed, a treadmill in the corner, and a display case lined with racing models of the Interstellar Mega Race. All these were gifts from Ulit.

The walls were covered with photos of drivers and video posters of racing highlights. The Mega Race was broadcast on their television, but Melgera was too small a planet to ever participate in it. With their underdeveloped technology, the very thought of it would be simply ridiculous.

Joe walked over to a video poster of last year's competition. Ludi Star, Colton Proud, and Stivella Lou took the top three places. They were awarded by Elira Bright, daughter of the president of the interstellar racing committee. Joe loved her face so much. It was calm and full of light. He could look at her for hours. She smiled and handed Ludi Star the medal. Joe pressed a button and entered the code in the pop-up window. Now Elira rewarded him, not Ludi. He laughed.

He heard a knock, and the door opened. It was Ulit. Joe sighed and lay down on the bed with his legs crossed.

"What did she say?" he asked laughing. "That I'm a waste of space?" Ulit nodded.

"That I am a disgrace to this family and going nowhere?" Ulit nodded again.

"And, oh wait," Joe touched his temples, "I have to go back to the Gurt ghetto?" He laughed.

"But you can't, right?"

The smile faded from Joe's face. And how did his brother always know everything about him?

"It's just one race. It's nothing."

Ulit sat down on the edge of the bed and smiled warmly like a father.

Joe felt a lump rising up in his throat and all the stress of the day was ready to burst out. If it wasn't for that meerkat...

"In my speech today," Ulit interrupted his thoughts, "I spoke about the fact that we need powerful funding from the Interstellar Committee in order to somehow correct the situation."

"Yes, but they don't even let us in," Joe replied, crossing his arms over his chest.

"They didn't. But I changed that," said Ulit proudly, "I did. That's what I said in today's speech if you would have listened."

Joe's eyes lit up.

"Wow! Look! My big brother is doing big things!" He was genuinely happy for him.

Ulit blushed slightly and adjusted his glasses.

"Of course, I don't know what they decide," he drawled. "But just imagine! For the first time in history, they're giving us twenty-seven minutes for a formal funding request."

"And how did you do it?" Ulit's face lit up.

"It's a long story, but the point is, there are four districts of Orion, right? Maldoran, Grathea, Dormart and X2. I proved that Melgera is a part of the Maldoran District! This was mentioned in the Chronicles of 17149 in article 7754. It was on its map. This means we are a part of it. Right?"

Joe nodded.

"So, they should listen to us and..." Ulit stammered when he saw that Joe yawning. "You're not interested, are you?"

"Of course I am," Joe assured him. "I just don't care about this planet. To be honest, I don't care about anything at all!"

Ulit's face froze as if he had been hit in the forehead. He thought for a moment.

"Our water is nearly gone," he said getting up. "We have half a year or a year left, no more. And if I don't get funding tomorrow..."

Joe yawned again. Ulit sighed.

"Mother said she'll kick you out tomorrow if you don't sign up for the water treatment work."

.

Joe nodded as his brother was about to leave

"Ulit," he called out to him. "It is not your fault. I mean…me. Don't take on too much, okay? Only saving the planet, nothing more."

Ulit stretched his lips into a thin line.

"There are things you should try," he said.

"For example?" Joe chuckled.

"For example, to live and think like Orans."

Ulit carefully closed the door as he left the room.

Chapter 5

Chance

"Today, for the first time in seventy-four years, the Interstellar Committee opened a portal for a delegation led by Ulit Dee Myers and allowed them into its domain to discuss the issue of financing the water supply on Melgera and to demand what, to quote the Minister of Interplanetary Relations, 'has long been ours.' At this actual moment the fate of our planet is being decided…"

The sound of the morning news on the screen above the bed was too loud. Joe opened his eyes and pulled the pillow over his head. He reached for the screen and turned off the sound, but at that moment his eyes met the gaze of his mother, who was standing over him. He turned away.

"Get up now," she said, pulling the blanket off him. "From this day on, you will pay for housing with earnings from the water treatment plant!"

Joe rolled off onto the floor and crawled under the bed. But his mother began to grab racing cars from the stand and throw them at him. He immediately jumped up, trying to catch them before they fell.

"What are you doing?!" he yelled. "They cost a fortune!"

"Nobody needs this garbage except you."

She threw another dozen cars on the floor and left the room.

Joe had never been angrier. He threw on a long-sleeved shirt and ran out of the house just to get away from it.

From the platform at the end of their street, the Lower City could be seen. Joe knew he couldn't go back there, at least not now, not so soon. They had not yet forgotten his defeat. "What if, for once in your life, you follow Ulit's advice and try to live like an Oran?" he thought.

Joe reluctantly turned to the Upper City and went towards the water treatment facility.

There, they hired everyone who could not find a place in life. Not everyone was lucky with a brother like his. They were given jobs but were paid almost nothing. Although some would say it was a good way to start.

Joe approached the tall, square building and entered through doors that slid into the ceiling. A reception desk was visible near the far wall, where a queue lined up. He cast his eye over them. Two guys his

age and three old men. The racer glanced at the exit, but the doors had already come back down.

When he got to the front of the queue, he was able to see through a small window at the counter. A young girl sat typing quickly at her keyboard, entering information about new employees. Her dyed, faded hair was pulled back into a hastily gathered bun, and her fingernails showed orange lacquer that was chipped here and there. She chewed gum and yawned every now and then, hiding behind piles of applications.

When she saw Joe she chuckled. The young man leaned on the counter.

"Hi there."

"Your arm," the girl said, trying to sound stern.

"Is it necessary?"

The girl giggled and twisted a lock of her hair.

"If you don't show your arm, I won't register you."

Joe slowly lifted his sleeve, proudly revealing the bird-lizard tattoo.

"A Gurt?" the girl looked disappointed. "We have too many of them today."

She shook her head. "Next."

But Joe didn't move.

"Do you know who my brother is?" he asked, smiling sweetly.

The girl frowned.

"Ulit Dee Myers"

She thought for a moment, and then tapped on the keyboard.

"Wait, is that the one who went to the Interplanetary Committee of Orion today?"

"That's the guy."

The girl stared at the screen again in disbelief, and then at the racer. Joe nodded.

"Okay, okay, put this on." She threw him a bag with a uniform. "Go to the room 503 on the left."

Joe winked at her, and she giggled again.

The clean water didn't smell very good, but the dirty water smelled truly terrible. They were even given nose-clips! Needless to say, it was impossible to endure even a few minutes there, let alone a twelve-hour shift. But leaving right away would have been like calling himself a wimp, so Joe held on.

One hour, two, three. On the tenth hour, he started counting minutes. Then his patience snapped. "To hell with all this," he thought, pulled off his wet uniform, and approached the register.

"Couldn't you have lasted a couple of hours more?" the girl drawled disappointedly. "You poor thing. Payment is only at the end of the shift."

Joe glared at her in disapproval.

"Your brother will not help you with this," she said, and slammed the window in his face.

"Well, all right." The racer threw his hands in the air. "To hell with you all! All Orans! I didn't really want to do this anyway!" he yelled so loudly that his words echoed back at him.

Joe left and spent what was left of the day, hanging around. But when darkness came, without much thought, he headed towards the Lower City.

As he approached, he felt relieved. There was his world and life, which was to his liking. If only Ike would agree to lend him at least some old banger. If it's got wheels, he knows how to take it from there.

As he entered, he rolled up his sleeve and caught the eye of two men. They smoked cigarettes and seemed to watch him.

Ike's house was nearby. After passing several buildings, Joe stopped at a small cottage. He touched the "For Sale" sign and knocked.

Joe heard an old man's shuffling footsteps before he appeared on the threshold. But just as Joe wanted to enter, Ike blocked his way. He tried to close the door, but Joe put his foot in the way.

"Come on, Ike," the racer said. "We had a fight, but you know you need me!"

"Not anymore," Ike said firmly. "I already have a dozen potential clients like you. But I'll bet on any of them, rather than you, number two."

"We both know I'm number one," Joe said resentfully.

"There's something you need to understand about yourself," Ike said, choosing his words.

Joe was all attention.

"In big things, you will always be number two. No matter how hard you try. Not because you're a bad racer or a bad kid... You just don't have what it takes to be first. That's what I realized."

"Nonsense!"

"I have an instinct for such things. Maybe it's luck or fate, but you won't become a legend."

Ike pushed Joe's leg hard with his walking stick and slammed the door in his face.

Joe sighed. Where will he go now? He didn't have any money. Even if Ike refused him, no mechanic would want to do business with him again.

He stepped out onto the dusty road. Above, the lights of the Upper City shone. But he was not welcomed there either.

"What happened, Joe? You don't know where to go?" He heard a voice ask.

The two men who were watching him were getting closer.

"Do you think that by rolling up your sleeve you can change where you belong?"

"Do I know you?" Joe took a step back. "No. But everyone knows you."

"Okay, okay." Joe raised his hands, stepping back. "I understand. You made bad bets."

"That's for sure. But there is more." One of them grabbed Joe by the collar.

"Can't even imagine what," breathed out the racer. "Who paid you to lose?"

"Nobody! I swear!" Joe tried to escape his grip.

"Leave him," said the second. "After all, he used to be our hero once". The man pushed him away and the racer fell to the ground.

"Joe Dee Myers," he said contemptuously. "You are not a Gurt, and you don't deserve to be."

He spat and turned away.

Joe breathed a sigh of relief as they moved away from him. Why did they all think he lost on purpose? Though he had enough enemies who could spread these rumors.

News reports rang on his bracelet, and Joe remembered that he had completely forgotten about his brother. He pressed a button, and a screen appeared in the air in front of him. It was a conference with a returning delegation.

Ulit looked even more pale and upset than usual.

"We were denied funding," he said curtly and left the hall.

Joe turned off the screen and looked up at the night sky. At least he wasn't the only one who felt like a failure. He got up and headed home because he had nowhere else to go.

In the dining room, the lights were on, as was always in the evenings. Ulit and Sheila dined in silence. Joe decided to join them. An idea popped into his head, which seemed amazing to him, and he wanted to share.

"Ulit, Mother," he said, breaking into a smile as he sat down at the table.

Sheila was so upset that she didn't even look in his direction. But Ulit, although sad, smiled at him, as always.

"There won't be any water," Joe said cheerfully.

"Is that right?" Mom looked up at him sternly.

"Is that a reason for joy?"

"It is a reason to leave this planet!"

His eyes blazed as if he had said something that could solve all their problems. But Sheila didn't seem to be happy about it.

"There will be no water. This means that the whole planet will come to an end!"

"Well, to hell with it!" said Joe. "Who needs it anyway?"

"To hell with it? Billions of lives!"

"Yes, to hell with them all! Why don't we just get out of here and that's it?"

They argued in raised tones until they started yelling at each other.

Ulit raised his hands up and they fell silent. He carefully wiped his mouth with a napkin and looked at them.

"The Interplanetary Committee of Orion is located on the artificial planet Agarna," he said calmly.

"Wow!" Joe said with feigned enthusiasm, as if he didn't know.

"And the committee building itself is as big as a city. There are millions of entrances and exits, rooms and halls. We were given twenty- seven minutes for our report, but we spent twelve hours there waiting."

"AND?"

"I walked through many halls where only the planets of Orion have access. But not us."

Joe began yawning. Everything that Ulit said always seemed so boring to him.

Ulit, as if on purpose, took a fork and began to stick a pea with it. It took a long time, but he succeeded.

"There was one hall there," he said.

"Hall of boring stories?"

"The Mega Race Lottery Hall."

"Why would that matter now?" asked Sheila. But Joe's attention became crystal clear.

Participants of the Mega Race were chosen in two ways. There were one hundred of them in total. The recruitment of the first half-fifty "professionals", was competitive and included professional racers making significant success in the universe.

The second half, who were called the "lucky ones," were selected using a lottery and absolutely everyone could participate, although the competition was incredibly huge. All this took place in the Interstellar Committee on planet Agarna, where the races were held, like many other interstellar events of Orion.

"I added his name into the draw," Ulit said simply and calmly ate the pea on his fork.

There was a mental pause in Joe's mind.

"Ha! Haha!" He ruffled his curly hair, then froze in shock, coming back to his senses when Sheila laughed a cheerful, almost childish laugh, which he had not heard from her for a long time. Joe joined her, followed by Ulit. They all ended up laughing for a long time.

"Any visitor of the Interplanetary Committee can enter a name, can you imagine?" Ulit said. "That's why it is almost impossible to get there!"

Joe got up and began to walk around the table in circles.

"I am participating in the Mega Race lottery! Seventh Star! Ulit, this is the best gift I can imagine."

He pounded on the table as they continued to laugh.

"I am participating in the Interstellar Mega Race looot-teeer-ryyy! Of course, there are usually about a million participants, and only fifty "lucky ones" are chosen. Chances are almost zero. But oh my, this is so cool!"

Joe was jumping and beaming with happiness. "This is the best day of my life!"

"Noooooo," drawled Ulit, "this is our chance." Joe stopped.

"Chance?"

"If you are chosen, and if you win, there will be enough money to finance the water supply for ten planets like ours."

"Ahh."

A chain of events and a possible future flashed through his head. "You thought I did it for you?" said Ulit laughing.

"Well," Joe got up. "Anyway, the chances are zero. And even if I win the lottery, your committee will ban me for the same reasons they denied funding. And even if they approve me, I won't be able to win the race, that's nonsense. But, Ulit, thanks! You are the best!"

Joe winked at him, got up and, whistling his favorite song, went to his room.

He lay in bed for a long time and could not sleep, thinking that all beautiful things were beyond reach. He looked through the window at the night sky, where the stars shone so brightly, and then extended his hand to one of them. But alas, it was so far away.

"No, that's impossible," Joe thought.

After all, they were on Melgera, a small planet at the very edge of Orion. Luck does not come to such backwaters. Their destiny is only to dream about the things they can't ever achieve.

At this moment, he even understood his brother and his hopeless struggle for their planet, which, as it seemed, nobody could help.

He continued to look at the stars for a long time. They could not see him at all, but the ghostly moons walked across the sky and seemed to shed their light through the window on purpose, preventing him from falling asleep.

"No, that's impossible," Joe thought again. He turned away and then fell asleep.

Chapter 6

Who's Joe Dee Myers?

Something rumbled very loudly. And this sound pulled Joe out of such sweet dreams.

"Who is Joe Dee Myers?" asked the announcer from the screen. "Today, the Interstellar Committee of Orion contacted the Committee of Foreign Relations of planet Melgera for the first time to report amazing and I would say incredible news, namely that one of the inhabitants of our planet for the first time in history was included in the list of "lucky ones" and became a participant of the annual Interstellar Mega Race of Orion. How he got there is still a mystery. But now everyone is asking only one question, who is he? Who is Joe Dee Myers?"

Joe reached for the screen to turn off the sound but froze and opened his eyes, not believing what he was hearing. It didn't seem to be a dream. The announcer continued.

"Is he a Gurt or an Oran? Lirta, do you have anything on that?"

"No, Pin, it is not clear," the girl answered. "According to our latest data, he participated in the races of the Gurts, although he is listed within the Oran districts."

"A Gurt? Are we talking about their amateur races? How interesting. The case is unprecedented! But how is he going to participate, and will he?"

Ulit and Sheila ran into the room.

"You got in! You got into the Mega Race! You're "lucky," Joe," they shouted.

But Joe still couldn't believe it.

"Seventh star! But there were more than a million candidates," he said to himself. "And only fifty were chosen."

The bracelet on his arm kept making ringing sounds. Joe pressed it. Numbers swirled on the screen that appeared in mid-air next to his face.

"Three million subscribers?! Seventh Star! Yesterday there were less than five thousand!"

The numbers kept adding up.

Ulit jumped on the bed, which was not typical of him at all, and Sheila clapped her hands.

They stopped when there was a noise outside the windows. Ulit looked out.

"Reporters," he said. "A lot of them."

"Seventh Star," was all Joe could say.

Ulit adjusted his glasses and became serious.

"We must prepare."

"For what?" Joe got up and put on his clothes "We have neither the money nor the resources to participate in the race."

"Exactly." Ulit grabbed him by the shoulders. "We must get funding for participation and everything that is required. This is a lot for us, but not for the planet. You should ask for race funding for the sake of the planet's water supply."

"But how is this connected?"

"In the most direct way! They will invest money in you only for the sake of a higher goal."

Car horns sounded outside the window, and Joe involuntarily felt a wave of something like fear or electric current go down his back.

"It's all about the correct presentation of information," said Ulit. "You must know what you are doing and why you are doing it!"

"Right," Joe nodded without really giving it much thought.

"And no more 'I do not care about everyone and everything!'" Sheila said.

"Ok, I get it, I get it now," Joe replied.

He cautiously approached the window and pulled back the curtain, but immediately jumped back. Dozens of cameras had already captured this moment.

Joe hid behind the bed, but Ulit tossed him a dusty racing jacket and pushed his brother out of the room.

"Go, Joe, go. You must make your first statement."

The racer went down the stairs and stopped at the door. His knees were shaking, but at the same time he was experiencing the same feeling that he had every time before the races, the excitement and desire to achieve what the crowd that passionately believed in him wanted.

He took a deep breath, opened the door, and smiled as widely as he could.

Dozens of cameras and drones hovered in the air looking at him from all sides. Joe waved his hand in all directions.

"Are you Joe Dee Myers?" came a female voice from a small crowd of reporters.

"I am." Joe straightened his jacket and winked at her. "And ready to race like never before in my life."

"How long have you been racing?"

"I was born in a racing car!"

The reporters laughed.

"Are you a Gurt? Orans have not practiced racing for a very long time."

"I'll teach them," he said. "Easy."

Another sound of approval.

"Why did you decide to participate in the Interstellar Mega Race?"

"Uh," Joe scratched his head. "The planet, you know...uh, water. We have water problems, don't we?"

They waited for more, but Joe just shrugged it off, as if they should have figured it out on their own.

"Where will you get sponsors? Participation is very expensive, and it is amost impossible to win."

"I thought you'd help me with this," Joe said irritably. There was a slight hum of disappointment.

Ulit peered out from behind the door, grabbed his arm, and dragged him back into the house.

"What?"

Joe was breathing excitedly, as if he'd just come from a run. "Calm down."

"Did I say something wrong?"

"For your first time, it was good but remember your public speeches will be broadcast on almost every living planet in the universe."

"Right."

"From now on, I will write speeches for you. All you must do is learn them, okay?"

"Fine," Joe replied.

"I've got fourteen minutes for your speech at the Ministry of Interplanetary Relations. You'll need to convince them, alright?"

Joe became sad as he watched the reporters leave. "Do you think they liked me?"

"You shouldn't think about that. There's only three days before the race.

This means that we have almost no time to find sponsors and a coach who will teach you everything."

His phone rang.

"Oh no," Ulit said after reading the message. "The Interstellar Committee of Orion doubts the legitimacy of your participation in the Mega Race."

"So, we already lost." Joe made a helpless gesture and fell on the sofa. He knew that something would spoil this endless holiday in his soul and would not give him what he so passionately wanted.

"No, not lost. It just means you must convince them too."

Joe jumped up and looked out the window. Reporters left. The road in front of him was clear and yet there were so many obstacles. What if he wasn't able to? He remembered Ike's words. Maybe he really did not have what was required. But he pushed those thoughts away.

"Now what?" he asked. "Should I hide?"

"On the contrary." Ulit shook his head, handing him a piece of paper. "Go to the city - to the Upper, then to the Lower - and tell them this."

Joe ran his eyes over the text.

"Get as much attention as you can and leave the rest to me. With any luck, tomorrow we'll go with a request to Agarna."

As he was leaving, Sheila touched his cheek.

"I might have been strict with you," she said, "but I always believed in you, Joe."

That gave him the same feeling that he experienced when received the love of the crowds, and he never felt happier.

"Go and show them."

She opened the door and pushed the racer out.

Chapter 7

The Moment of Glory

Joe looked around. There were no reporters. Had they lost interest in him so quickly? He looked up and immediately noticed how several drones hovered nearby. That made him feel better.

Where would he go? To the Lower City? What would he tell them? How would they treat him now that he was a participant of the Mega Race? Joe's entire life up until that moment flashed in his mind's eye. This chance was all he had left.

What would have happened if he had not woken up that morning to the sound of the news, where everyone was talking only about him? Without it, his life would be at an impasse. He did not know what would happen next, but he was clearly aware that he could not miss this opportunity and return to what was before.

He was walking out of his quarter when suddenly, someone called out to him.

"Joe? Joe Dee Myers?"

The racer turned. A boy of about ten pulled his mother by the hand and approached him.

"Mom, this is a participant of the Interstellar Mega Race that everyone is talking about."

Joe straightened his jacket.

"Hi!"

"Joe, will you give me an autograph?"

He took out a tablet, which, along with a pen, hovered in the air. Joe signed. The boy pressed the button on his jacket and a smiling Joe's face appeared on it.

"Now you're my idol, Joe." The racer winked at him.

"And how did you manage to get in?" the woman asked.

"Ma'am, I didn't have a choice," Joe said in his most serious air. "Our planet is in danger."

"Really?"

"Don't you know? Water resources are depleted, and the Interstellar Committee of Orion has refused to help us. By winning the Mega Race, I'll get funding for water supply for Melgera."

The woman raised her eyebrows in surprise.

"I didn't know it was that bad."

Joe shook his head.

"Well, I don't want to take any more of your time, ma'am, but please tell everyone you know, not about me, but about the water problem on Melgera, alright?"

"Of course." She pressed the button on her bag. Joe's face appeared on it, and the inscription below it read "I'm doing this for the sake of water on Melgera."

"Thank you," Joe said, putting his palms together and waving to the boy before moving on.

"Joe, you are a hero!" the boy shouted after him. "I will root for you!"

"Seventh star!" Joe said to himself. He was recognized. People turned around and walked towards him. First one or two, then there were more. Soon a crowd of Orans gathered around him. And to all of them, Joe said the same thing that he learnt from the text about water, written by his

brother.

"Joe! Joe! Joe!" soon the crowd chanted. "Give us the water!"

There were more and more drones around him and after a few hours a screen with a smiling Joe appeared on the building of the central square. He suddenly became serious and said, "I'm doing this for the sake of water on Melgera."

"Just think, a sixteen-year-old boy will fight a hundred participants from mega-developed planets in the Interstellar Mega Race and will not do it for the sake of winning. No, he will do it for the water on Melgera," announcers and reporters on all channels said. "You knew the water problem was that serious, Lirta?"

"No, Pin," the girl shook her head. "We all grew up knowing that there is this problem, and apparently that's why we got used to ignoring it instead of doing something."

"And the Interstellar Committee of Orion?"

"They refused to help."

The announcers shook their heads.

"It's good that we have Joe Dee Myers."

"Now this is our only hope."

As he approached the Lower City, he looked at his status: twelve million subscribers. But before he had entered the gates, the Gurts surrounded him and raised him in their arms. They made a din, whilst the crowd around him grew larger and larger.

"Jooooe! Jooooe! Jooooe! Dee! Dee! Dee! Myyyyyyyers!!!"

It seemed that all the Gurts on the planet had gathered here. They forgot about his failure and the fact that they all lost money betting on him. All that mattered now was that he would be in the Mega Race and they would become a part of it in a way.

In their arms, they carried Joe to the ground in front of the Star stadium, chanting like so many times before.

"Jooooe! Jooooe! Jooooe! Dee! Dee! Dee! Myyyyyyyyers!!!"

The racer enjoyed the moment. His face was on all the banners and screens of the stadium next to the clips of past Mega Race videos.

They brought him onto the stage. Joe raised his hand, and the crowd got became quiet, waiting for what he would say.

"Today I want to talk to you about water," said Joe as seriously as he could. "And about our dear and beloved planet, Melgera!"

The roar of adoration and admiration filled the stadium again, preventing him from continuing. Looking at this, Joe realized that even he himself did not expect this from Gurts.

"Give us back the water, Joooe! Bring back the water!" they shouted.

These were the ones who never cared about anything, and they taught him to be proud of it.

Going backstage, Joe opened the channel with the news.

"A wave of love, and, I would even say, hope, swept the stadium in the quarter of the Gurts, where Joe appeared today. But look at the rest of the cities on the planet," said the announcer. "Gurts and Orans, they all chant his name. It seems that today the whole planet has gathered to express support for Joe Dee Meyers and hope for his victory."

Joe laughed boyishly as he saw the crowds of Gurts and Orans embracing together. But when he looked up, he saw Ike. The mechanic looked sad and a little guilty.

"They're chanting your name again, aren't they?" he said.

Limping, he took a few more steps and sat down next to the young man. Without any hesitation Joe hugged him tightly.

"This is a chance for us, my dear Ike. Don't you understand? There, on Agarna, I'll need a mechanic."

But the old man only grunted in response and coughed, and then took out a handkerchief, wiping his beard and shaking his head.

"No," he said. "My career is in the past. Now I can only watch the stars." He pointed at the sky with his cane. "Besides, I don't understand anything about their cars, only about the insides of old Gurt bangers."

"Come on." Joe lightly pushed his shoulder. "Just imagine how much money we'll win! I'll give you a million times more than what I owe you."

But the old man looked at one point for a few moments, and then turned to him.

"Noi," he said. "That's who you need."

"Who?" Joe would only remember him when the alien was actually there in person.

"Only few people know," continued Ike, lowering his voice. "But Noi is from another planet. A very advanced one, like your Agarna! And there he was a mechanic in some incredibly important organizations." The old man waved his hands. "And when he came here, he had to retrain and work with Gurt cars. He once told me that here he feels like he lives among the ants and fixes their twigs. Can you imagine?"

Joe laughed and couldn't stop because this seemed just too incredible to him. At that moment, he noticed Noi who seemed to be hiding in the distance. He was peeking around the corner every now and then to steal a glance at the racer.

"Why is he so afraid of me?" Joe asked.

"He saw a great future in you when I didn't, so he will suit you much better."

"Don't talk like that, Ike."

The old man stood up, hugged the boy once more, and headed for the exit.

"I wish you victory," he said. "No, really, forget everything that I told you before. Just remember that this…" he pointed to the noisy stadium, "is a moment of glory that you have yet to earn."

Joe looked at him sadly and his heart seemed to ache, but the noise of the crowd was too loud to be ignored.

"Nooooiii," Joe shouted.

The alien looked around the corner, as if not believing that his name was being called, but when he was certain the racer was looking at him, he came forward.

"Noi knows absolutely everything about Mega Race racing cars. They may have two, or even one hundred and forty-four wheels, engines on the right, in front and in the back. And I could write a whole library about the degree ratio. Even a beginner's guide!"

"Degree ratio?" Joe frowned.

"Well, yes," answered Noi. "Why do you think their cars fly? It's all about this."

"All right," Joe replied. "You're hired."

"What?"

Noi couldn't believe it and his eyes suddenly became three times bigger, but he immediately pulled himself together and returned them to their previous size when he noticed that the racer almost jumped out of his skin.

"Noi is only trying to look like you, humans," the mechanic explained.

"Ahh, I see," said Joe. "Be ready by 7:45 tomorrow. We go to the Committee of Melgera, and then, if we're lucky, to Agarna."

He stepped back into the stadium and raised his arms above his head.

"In the name of water!" he shouted as loudly as he could, revealing his tattoo of a bird-lizard. "In the name of Melgera! And all the planets of periphery!"

The crowd repeated with a deafening scream:
"In the name of water! In the name of Melgera!"
Then everything was drowned in their incessant chanting: "Jooooo! Jooooe! Jooooe! Dee! Dee! Dee! Myyyyyyyers!!!"

Chapter 8

That Bird-Lizard

"Well done," was the first thing Joe heard when he opened his eyes in the morning. Ulit was standing over him.

It was early and the dissolving pink light of the scarlet moons flickered outside the window. Joe turned away, burying his nose in the pillow. He did not remember how he returned home yesterday. Perhaps the crowd carried him.

But Ulit took the pillows then pulled off the blanket.

"Today is the most important day of your life," Ulit said.

Reality returned to its place again. How sweet it was. Even sweeter than his dreams. Joe sat up in bed and looked at his bracelet, which just kept blinking.

"Five billion subscribers?!" Joe shook the bracelet, thinking it might be broken.

"Not surprising. Your speeches about water have been broadcast throughout the universe."

"So, these are subscribers from other planets?" he exclaimed.

"I got us time," said Ulit. "Meeting with the Committee of Melgera at 7:75. Meeting with the Committee of Orion at 17:50. Lilac portals, which is very good!"

"Yeah," Joe's head was spinning, "and then?"

"If we get funding, we need to find a mechanic and a coach."

"We got the mechanic," said the racer, rubbing his temples.

"Really? Ok," Ulit answered shortly, but with disbelief. "But the coach will cost us a fortune."

"I'll tell him about the water. It will be no problem."

"Well," Ulit adjusted his glasses. "Let's focus on financing and legitimizing of your participation first."

"Right," Joe agreed, falling back onto the bed.

But Ulit dragged him to the floor and then began to rummage through his wardrobe, picking out the best racing suit.

"You have to look like racing is your life."

"Don't I look like that all the time?"

Joe stood in front of the mirror, exposing the bird-lizard tattoo and waving to the imaginary crowd.

"We have to learn and rehearse the text," said Ulit, giving him a stack of paper sheets.

Joe ran his eyes over the text.

"Seventh Star! I can't even read half of the words here!"

They entered the kitchen, where Sheila greeted them with breakfast.

"So," said Ulit, pointing to the text. "Retell your life's story, drawing particular attention to your belief you held since childhood that water should be without dust."

"Shouldn't it?"

"Then you tell how you decided to become a racer in order to somehow help the water treatment organizations."

"Ha, I even worked there!" Joe said proudly.

"Right! It needs to be added." Ulit crossed out and amended a few sentences. "And then you tell them how you asked me to add your name to the lottery just to win and earn money for water supply for Melgera."

"Ah, ok."

Joe drank a glass of Kuraza juice, a fruit from the steppe that he found especially delicious today, and stood up, stretching.

"I'm ready."

At that moment, there was a knock on the door.

"Our mechanic," Joe explained. "Do you mind if he's on the team? A reliable man. That is, not actually a human. But come on, he is just like one of us."

Sheila opened the door and Noi appeared on the threshold. He looked as humanoid as possible. The suit was brand new, the thin hair on the head was combed and styled with gel, and in the hand was a small suitcase.

"Noi knows absolutely everything about the cars of the Mega Race," he said immediately instead of greeting. "Their engines decide half of the matter, and the rest is a degree ratio, but do not forget, of course, about simple mechanics. It's usually what fails first."

Ulit and Sheila looked at each other.

"Hey, Noi, chill," Joe said, spinning in his chair. "You're already hired."

The alien came in and sat on his suitcase in the corner, trying to be inconspicuous.

"Noi knows absolutely everything about the cars of the Mega Race," he muttered under his breath. "Absolutely everything."

"Nice to meet you," said Ulit. "Well, I think it's time for us to hit the road."

He turned to Joe.

"We will go through the portal, which will be opened to us in 2 minutes," he said.

Noi could hardly keep his eyes still, but he tried very hard.

Fortunately, by this time the portal had opened, and Ulit, waving goodbye to Sheila, almost pushed Noi and Joe inside.

Before they even blinked an eye, they found themselves in a bright hall with many seats lined up in rows. They were met by several Orans dressed in uniforms, the same that Ulit always wore.

"Ha," said Joe, "I always thought those were your home pajamas."
"Request 7894," Ulit said to the girl who approached them.

"Sit down," she said.

"This is the Waiting Room," Ulit explained. "We will spend several hours here. During this time, you will have time to learn the speech."

Joe looked around the room. It was full of people: old, young, respectable and not so much. They all waited their turn and were busy with their own affairs.

Joe thought that he was expected here and would be greeted with congratulations and applause right from the doorstep. But no one seemed to recognize him. Nobody even looked in his direction and nobody cared. This shook his self-confidence a little, and he pulled his sleeve down so that no one would see the bird-lizard tattoo.

Several hours passed and Joe fell asleep. In a dream, he saw Elira Bright. She walked around the millions of participants of the Mega Race of all past years, greeted them, smiled her soft feminine smile, and shook hands with them. But when she saw him, she stopped and made a wry face.

"Gurt? We do not invite Gurts here!"

All the members turned to Joe and gave him scornful looks. The racer took a step back, covering his tattoo. But he got tired. He stood up, straightening up proudly, and looked defiantly into their eyes.

"I am the bird-lizard itself!" he said so loudly that the whole universe could hear him.

And unexpectedly for him, he saw how his skin was covered with feathers and scales. He grew a beak and rose so high above the participants that he covered them with his endless shadow. And next to him on both sides appeared the same bird-lizards like him. The one on the right turned his head and said:

"There is no going back, Joe. These are the rules."

At that moment, he woke up from Ulit prodding him on the shoulder. "Our turn," he said, tugging his elbow.

Noi grabbed him too, helping to push and pull him along.

"Thanks, Noi. I can handle it myself," Joe said, stifling a yawn.

They were led into a small room, in which a lot of screens with the faces of the ministers hung over the dais. Joe thought that they were as gray and dull as Ulit. He chuckled as he thought what would happen if he told them that he was the bird-lizard itself. But at that moment Ulit whispered to him, as if reading his thoughts:

"Do not deviate from the text."

Joe nodded and stepped out onto the dais.

"Are you Joe Dee Myers?" asked the woman on the screen.

"Yes, that's me," Joe replied and smiled his most charming smile. "Does your brother Ulit Dee Myers work for the Committee?"

"He does, ma'am."

"Did you win the participation in the Mega Race of Orion?"

Joe nodded, wondering where to start giving a prepared speech. But the man on the screen also began to ask questions.

"You caused a sensation by declaring that you will give the winning prize to finance Melgera's water supply?"

"That's right."

"What are the guarantees?"

"Of a victory?"

"No, that you will give money for water."

"Seventh Star!" Joe made a helpless gesture. "I promise!"

But he immediately met Ulit's gaze and guessed he should start his speech:

"Ever since childhood, I felt the taste of dust in the water and…" "Have you ever raced outside the Gurt Star stadium?"

The racer felt helpless.

"The fact that you won the lottery is an accident. The chances of you winning are close to zero," they monotonously said one after the other. "The budget does not allow us to participate in lotteries or rely on ghostly odds. Request denied."

Joe was so shocked that he just stood silently. Ulit ran to his rescue.

"We are asking for very little," he said. "Only funding for a car and a coach. We already have a mechanic!"

Noi ran out onto the pedestal. He breathed deeply and obviously wanted to say something, but could not, silently opening and closing his mouth.

"He knows absolutely everything about the cars of Mega Race!" Joe said instead of him.

At that moment, a feeling of anger and protest arose in him. How could they refuse him when everyone else believed in him so much?

"My brother sought funding from the Interstellar Committee itself!" he said so that he drowned out all the voices in the hall. "He proved that Melgera is part of some Orion district! He added my name to the Mega Race Lottery! And all for the sake of that water! Can't you give me just one chance to solve all your - yes, YOUR - problems?"

"Request denied."

"Your aspirations are worthy of respect. But your request is denied," the woman repeated sternly. "We do not play games with the universe."

"And I do play," shouted Joe. "Because I am the bird-lizard itself!"

Full of anger and indignation, he ran out of the hall. Ulit and Noi followed him.

◉ ◉

Chapter 9

The "Raging Kretrag" Tavern

Joe ran down the cold corridor, not knowing where he was going. His temples throbbed with a sense of injustice. They didn't even listen to him! They had decided everything before he even started talking! How would

he get back now? What would he say to all those who believed in him? And the water. It really did taste like dust!

"Don't worry, Joe," Noi said carefully. "You still have a meeting at the Interstellar Committee of Orion."

"They will never legitimize his participation without funding," said Ulit. "Moreover, they will not even allow him to present the request."

He walked over to Joe, who looked so upset he was about to cry, and gave him a fatherly hug.

"It's okay. You tried."

"Perhaps we will not be allowed to present the request," Noi reasoned, as if talking to himself. "But we will certainly be allowed to Agarna once the time in Interstellar Committee is appointed. We can take a walk and relax. There is one tavern named "Raging Kretrag." Noi was there a hundred years ago - a great place. Most of all, it is well known for the fact that some issues are resolved there in no time. Even the most difficult issues in the universe."

Ulit and Joe stared at him in surprise. "You've been on Agarna?"

"Noi is from the planet Olerda," the mechanic explained. "The water there is cleaner than in the springs of Gelvera and Fai. We are allowed everywhere without a single question. Noi has been on Agarna and everywhere in Orion a thousand times."

"Seventh star," was all Joe could say.

"Well," said Ulit, laughing and clapping Noi on the shoulder with joy. "Then let's try our luck one more time!"

Noi nodded with the air of a man who had already taken up his duties and was doing them well.

"But Noi has to warn you" he said. "Only special visitors are allowed in that tavern. For example, those with a star rating."

"How much is that?" Joe asked.

"Not less than seven billion."

Joe looked at his bracelet.

"How about seven and a half?"

Ulit and Noi stepped into a portal. Joe didn't even know how it happened, but he appeared in a completely new place. The first thing he noticed was that the ceiling was high, very high, and on it was a map of the starry sky with dots that flashed every now and then, marking the places from which new arrivals appeared. "Melgera," he read, and the dot sailed into the dark ocean, and then drowned in it, evaporating. There were a lot of aliens of the most different types, sizes, and attire.

"Don't look at them like that," Ulit whispered.

Joe noticed that they really answered him with cold looks, measuring him from head to toe.

"This is the Mall of Wonders," Noi explained. "Here, without tax, you can buy almost any product in the universe."

"But we don't have time for that," Ulit said.

"There," Noi pointed out. "The tavern will be on the left wing of the market."

They rushed forward, and Joe only managed to turn his head to glance over the goods that he had never seen in his life and could not even imagine.

When they stepped out onto the mini-portal track, which transported them hundreds of meters in an instant, Joe began to laugh like a child in an amusement park. He liked it so much that he did not want to leave, rushing a hundred meters forward and back, and then again and again. But Ulit decided best to tug him out of there.

Finally, they came to a massive white building that looked like the head of a monster with open jaws ready to eat them alive. Above the entrance was a sign, "Raging Kretrag."

"Who is Kretrag?" asked Joe.

"The most dangerous monster in the universe," replied Noi. "Why is everything written here only in our language?"

"It is written in all languages of the universe," explained Noi again. "Here, everything around you senses your energy background and adjusts to it automatically. Besides, we all had a chip built into us as kids, right? Noi doesn't think Melgera is an exception. This chip allows you to understand and speak most of the known languages of the universe."

Joe knew this, although he had not thought about it before because he had never been outside of his planet. However, he remembered there were few aliens on Melgera, and those he met, Joe understood perfectly well.

Ulit nervously adjusted his glasses and stopped in front of the entrance, but the doors did not open.

"The one with the star rating should go first," Noi explained.

Joe stepped forward. The doors opened, and they found themselves inside a spacious, noisy tavern.

The mind of the racer was not immediately able to capture what he saw. Tables with visitors were everywhere, but they seemed to be layered on top of each other, each existing in its own reality and in the world of the entire hall.

"Arnie, let them sit at the table 2915. They've been waiting here forever!" announced a big, blue-skinned woman on a speaker.

"On my way, Marla."

Tall Arnie with seven eyes, who had to bend his long neck in three arcs in order not to hit his head on the ceiling, approached them. Joe couldn't keep his eyes off his roller clad feet which enabled him to hover above the ground. "Before we start, I beg you, please," Arnie pleaded. "Do not write a bad review about me. It's so hard to get a job here, and I trained as a waiter at the most prestigious college in Chivra."

"A table for three," Noi said sternly.

"Of course, of course," Arnie fussed guiltily.

Joe didn't know how it happened, but they suddenly found themselves at the table as if everyone was gathered up and pushed through time and space.

"Aaah," said Arnie, "guests from Melgera! We haven't had such since 17475 according to the commonly accepted calendar, of course."

A screen appeared in front of him, on which Melgera's video flashed by at quadruple speed.

"Yeah ... yeah… periphery ... ha, interesting planet." Arnie continued, looking at the screen, "A rich history, wonderful people. And you're a racer." He pointed to Joe. "Wow! You are a participant of the Mega Race! Seven and a half billion is a good rating indeed!"

He turned and shouted as loud as he could.

"Marla, we have a Mega Race participant here!"

"Just announce it, dunderhead," she answered him as if from a parallel universe.

"Attention, attention." His voice was so loud that the whole universe probably heard. "Sitting at the table 2915, you will never believe it, a future racer of the Mega Race, Jooooe Dee Myyyyyyyyers himself!"

Joe's face at the moment of racing at the Star Stadium spun over all the tables in the tavern. It showed the moment when his car turned over and exploded, and then a close-up of a sand meerkat and a roaring stadium.

"Where did they get this video?!" Joe liked it so much that, forgetting everything, he clapped his hands.

Arnie touched his ear.

"Yeah, I understand. Of course."

"Customers from 1107 tables are willing to pay your bill for just one tiny little autograph, and a selfie, of course. Which table will you choose?"

Ulit was so surprised he couldn't say a word, and Noi cast annoyed glances at the waiter.

"557th," Joe said with a cheerful shake of his curls. "Wonderful!"

The three alien girls appeared immediately next to their table. They giggled and held out a bracelet to Joe that had a screen appearing above it.

"Okaaay," Joe signed. "It's so nice of you."

But they didn't listen. They stood behind him, preening and straightening their hair, then took a selfie and disappeared.

"Seventh Star!" Joe looked around, not wanting to believe that they left him so fast. "I just got a taste."

"Can we finally place an order?" Noi growled angrily.

"Of course, the gentleman from Olerda." Arnie opened the screen in front of him, wanting to read information about his planet, but Noi immediately closed it sharply. Arnie hunched over in embarrassment. "Sorry, I just wanted..."

"Koverki with Churyl sauce," Noi said angrily.

Koverki, whatever they were, immediately appeared in front of the mechanic, and he began to gobble them up with unbelievable speed.

"So...so...so..." Arnie cheered up again, turning to Joe and Ulit. "Melgera's kitchen! I can recommend something really good for you!"

"Nothing better than something out of the ordinary. Your choice," Ulit said politely.

"Of course! Arnie has great taste!"

Food and drink appeared right in front of them.

"Now I'll leave you," he said sweetly, "enjoy your dinner and don't forget to give me a good review."

He cast a guilty look at Noi and was about to leave but stopped.

"If you need anything, blink," said Arnie, blinking every one of his seven eyes, "and I'll be right here."

With these words, he disappeared.

"Should we ask him to announce that we need help?" asked Ulit.

"It won't be required." Noi was finishing eating the Koverki "Everyone in this hall knows already who we are and why we are here. Noi suggests launching a crowdfunding."

"Will they really agree to fund the race for another signature and selfie?" Joe asked in surprise.

"Perhaps," Noi shrugged. "Or perhaps it won't be necessary. You never know what to expect at this tavern."

He pressed his bracelet, and a camera appeared in front of Joe.

"Tell them why you came and what you need."

Joe hesitated for a moment, but then shook his curls and became serious.

"I won't say I'm the best racer in the universe, but I'm going to become one. And it's not just for fun. My planet desperately needs water! So, if you care, fund my races!"

He winked with a champion smile, showing the bird-lizard tattoo on his arm.

Arnie's face appeared in the air above the table.

"Crowdfunding has been launched," he said sweetly. "In front of you are the size of the donations."

As numbers swirled in the air Joe and Ulit laughed in disbelief and Noi was busy calculating something in his mind.

"Come on, come on," he repeated.

Joe and Ulit tasted the food, and both immediately agreed that it was the most delicious thing they had ever eaten in their lives. But before they finished their meal, the numbers stopped.

Noi took a sip of the drink that was on the table.

"Let's say that's enough for racing cars and their complete repairs." He sounded upset. "But even if they let us race, we need a coach, and for that this money is not enough."

"I can handle it myself," said Joe. "I've always done it myself. A lot of the racers of the Mega Race participated without a coach."

"And almost none of them even made it to the second round," Noi said.

"What does the coach do?" Ulit knew nothing about these matters.

"How can Noi explain this..." Noi drummed his fingers on the table. "The right coach makes a winner out of a racer. He manages the race as if he holds the steering wheel, and not the one who is driving. They say that it is the coach who wins the tournament, not the racer."

"And how expensive is he?"

"Very," answered Noi. "Without him there is no chance. Absolutely no chance!"

"Anyway, I think at this stage we have already won," said Ulit, getting up. "But there is no more time. The hearing will begin in 12 minutes."

They moved towards the exit, rushing through the expanding and contracting space again. And Joe, who was walking behind, danced and hummed his favorite song without a care.

Chapter 10

The Beauty of the Universe

◉

Noi rushed forward, occasionally crashing into passersby, and stopped at the entrance to a massive building, the top of which couldn't be seen.

Ulit breathed heavily and tried to say something to Joe, but it took him a few seconds to come to his senses.

"There's not much time left," he exhaled nervously. "Don't forget you have to convince these people that we're part of the Interstellar Community of Orion. Here."

He pointed to a place in the text of the speech.

"Focus on the 7754th article which says that even though we're a periphery, our planet was on Orion maps. And don't forget the water."

"Got it." Joe nodded.

They opened a portal and immediately found themselves somewhere completely different. All three sat in chairs that slowly hovered around, creating the feeling of flying.

Joe tried to get up and almost screamed; he found himself standing in mid-air. Ulit pulled him by his sleeve and sat him back down.

There was nothing around, only white space and seven creatures that were looking at the transparent screen in front of them with a soft smile. It showed Joe himself, fast-forwarding a speech that Ulit had prepared.

"But I haven't read it yet, have I?" went through Joe's head. However, he did not want to interrupt them.

"They're projecting the most likely future of the next fifteen minutes," Noi whispered.

"Article 7754." The beautiful thin woman shook her head and took a sip from a long cup with a straw, and then yawned sleepily.

"This is Ulka, the head of the committee," Noi whispered again. "She decides everything here."

The creatures listened to the end and closed the screen, looking at each other.

"I believe you will agree," said Ulit, adjusting his glasses. "We have valid reasons for legitimization of Joe's participation in the race."

The creatures all nodded at once, looking at him respectfully, then turned to each other.

"He is already on the 59th place in the rating among the participants," said one of the heads of the committee.

Joe opened his eyes wide in surprise.

"Yes, his popularity is growing even among the most significant planets of the community," agreed another. "All because of the water, of course."

"Refusal will cause discontent of too many. This can be seen as an action against the code of the Interstellar Committee," said the third.

Ulka leaned back in her chair, looking up into the white void.

"A small, insignificant planet of the periphery, without water or resources and not even in Orion's district. And now this boy is winning the Mega Race lottery. There is something beautiful about this situation. Too beautiful to ignore," she said.

"The beauty of the Universe is in its unpredictability," the alien sitting next to her remarked.

"Mmm." Ulka stretched again drowsily. "The boy is popular, but what are his real chances?"

"Considering his genetics, background, skills and other things, the chances of winning are…"

The screen lit up with the answer: 1.7%.

Ulka narrowed her eyes and took a sip of her smoothie. "Then why won't we increase the stakes?"

The faces of the aliens expressed interest.

"If the boy wins, we will bring the planet into the Orion district. It will have access to all events and funds."

"And if not?"

"No one will judge us for refusing to help."

At that moment, they disappeared. They simply vanished in front of Joe, who, along with Ulit and Noi, continued to soar in the white void. The screen reappeared in front of them. Ulit tensed up, adjusted his glasses, and read:

"Participation in races is legitimized under new conditions."

What followed was an endless list of everything that Melgera would get if Joe won.

They did not have time to read even a hundredth part of it before they were suddenly transported somewhere else.

It was a large pavilion with a wide, long road that stretched along the perimeter of the hall as far as the eye could see. The racing cars with the participants of the Mega Race were either racing in the air or standing around.

In front of the new arrivals, a short, chubby alien appeared with such a happy look, as if he had been waiting for them here all his life.

"Hello! Hello! I'm Tewie, the coordinator! Welcome to the territory of the Mega Race pavilion," he shouted, trying to drown out the noise around. "When I was informed about your arrival, I was infinitely happy! I said to myself, it's J-o-e D-ee Myyyyers himself!" He stopped in front of the racer and hugged him tightly. "You can't even imagine how everyone is waiting for you here! How many bets have already been made! You missed the first two press conferences, and they were only talking about you, your planet, and water! Wow!"

His hair suddenly stood on end for a brief moment and then settled back down again.

"Well, well!"

Joe just laughed, while Ulit stood at a loss, and Noi began to attack him with questions.

"Where is the dressing room? Where is the participants' hotel? When will we receive the car?"

"Wait, wait," said the bewildered Ulit. "Can you explain to us what is actually happening here?"

"The three of you must be in the territory of the Interstellar Mega Race town until the end of the competition," Tewie explained. "Those are the terms of your agreement with the Interstellar Committee. Here you can train as much as you want but please try to follow the rules and attend all the events."

"What is required of us right now?" Ulit asked.

"Today you have to register at the hotel and get a car, which, of course, is better to do with a coach."

"We don't have a coach," Noi muttered.

"Ah," Tewie gave them a sympathetic look. "Well in that case you're on your own! The pavilion maps are already loaded into your wristbands. Get started! And yes, orientation meeting tomorrow, and the day after tomorrow at 7:95, the first race."

With these words, he disappeared.

Noi opened the screen and started to read. Ulit continued to stand still, looking at the cars passing in front of him, unable to digest what was happening.

As for Joe, he froze in place staring at something. She stood not so far from him. Elira Bright. She was no longer a poster on the wall in his room. She was alive, real. The girl was talking to the racers. At some point, she turned and, meeting Joe's gaze, smiled softly. A wave of electric current passed through Joe's body.

"Hurry up, we need to sort out the car," Noi said, grabbing both brothers by the elbows. He dragged them forward. "Hotel", he shouted.

Less than a second passed before they appeared in a spacious lobby with a dark hall and decor in the style of the old universe.

"Local portals open here with the power of thought," Noi explained, seeing their puzzled faces. "You need to concentrate and say a code word, for example, "Hotel", and you'll be there."

He pressed his bracelet, and a map screen appeared in front of him. "We are located on the 315th floor. Room!"

They disappeared again and reappeared in a spacious mansion with a swimming pool, tennis court, and views of the best places in the universe that changed every five minutes.

"Seventh Star, Noi, who are you to know everything?" Joe jumped onto the soft downy carpet.

"Noi has been on Agarna many times, and elsewhere in the inhabited universe," said the alien proudly, looking through the artificial window. "Noi is one thousand and seventeen years old."

"What?"

Ulit and Joe looked at each other.

"And how did you get to Melgera and get stuck there?"

"It's a long story." The alien's face twisted. "But we'd better hurry. We have very little time before the first race, and Joe has never even sat behind the wheel of a real racing car."

"I'll stay here," said Ulit, sitting down on the sofa. "I am a little unwell from all this teleportation."

The next second Noi and Joe were standing in the car showroom pavilion.

"Seventh star!" Joe exclaimed, unable to believe what he was seeing.

Thousands of racing cars hung and spun in the air in miniature form, and in front of them were screens with information about manufacturers, assembly, parts availability, and general parameters. They were nothing like the primitive cars on Melgera or those that Ike constructed for Joe. These all had multiple wheels, engines, and gears.

Joe tapped the screen at random. To his surprise, the actual physical car immediately appeared in front of them.

He opened the door and sat inside.

There were hundreds of buttons, screens, switches, and levers in front of him, and Joe had no idea why they were there.

"At least I know how to turn the steering wheel," he giggled.

"You don't," Noi sighed with the look of an alien who could see so much work ahead of him. "The steering wheel should be turned only when all other parameters are set in the right ratio. All the wheels, engines, and turbines are adjusted in degree ratios, and only after that does the steering wheel turn. Each attribute in the car has a number and its functionality is determined by a degree from 1 to 1000. First you need to understand this, and also that there are many modes: riding, flying, sub aqua. Besides, this car doesn't suit us. Everything here is too automatic. Noi can't improve it."

Joe got out with a disappointed look. He imagined Elira Bright staring at him when he couldn't even turn the steering wheel and other racing cars moved forward, leaving him behind.

"How long does it take to master all this and bring it to perfection?" he asked.

"Your whole life is not enough," the alien answered. "But Noi will say this: Noi was very lucky that Joe Dee Myers made him his mechanic, so he will arrange everything for him in the best possible way."

The alien took out a small box, opened it, and with his two fingers, carefully removed a tiny device. Then he attached it to Joe's temple.

"Noi bought it when he was last on Olerda about a hundred years ago," he said. "The model is not the latest, but Noi updated the library for you."

"What is this?" Joe asked.

"Information transmitter. It uploads the contents of books, knowledge, and skills to your brain. Noi has downloaded one hundred and thirty-two thousand books and manuals on the technique of driving and fixing racing cars. Plus twenty-thousand car maneuvers. Noi only selected the best the night before. Also, another hundred thousand books about the inhabited universe. Just in case."

"Noi," Joe exclaimed. "What would I do without you?"

But in the next moment, somewhere in the background of his consciousness, a bright light flashed. Joe's legs buckled and he fell.

"The first time is always like this," exclaimed Noi in a scared voice.

"But maybe Noi shouldn't have uploaded all of it at once. Joe, are you alright?"

He was shaking the racer by the shoulders. "Joe, wake up, you can't die now, Joe!"

The racer opened his eyes and grabbed his temples. His head was spinning.

"I guess I'm alive," he answered and sat down. "Was I out for a long time?"

"Few seconds."

"I feel like I've been somewhere else for at least a month." Slowly, he got up. Noi gave a sigh of relief.

"For a moment, Noi thought he had actually killed Joe Dee Myers." Noi lowered another car and pushed Joe in it.

"And now?" he asked. "What do you see?"

For a few moments, Joe stared at the blank screens and buttons, but then unexpectedly, as if by rote memory, he turned them on, then pushed the levers and started the engines one by one. The information seemed to come to his brain from somewhere in his subconscious. It was as if he'd been driving these cars all his life.

"Seventh Star!" he exclaimed, slowly turning the steering wheel and moving the car back. "Now everything here makes sense."

Joe was now captivated by how easily he operated the car.

"If everything is so simple," he said as he entered the straight. "Why can't everyone participate in the race?"

"Everyone can participate," the mechanic replied. "But winning is another matter. Mega Race has many obstacles and unexpected situations where the car and knowledge are only two factors. Racers must be both genetically and energetically strong enough to pass all tests with maximum success. They risk their lives and many of them do not return. On the road, everything will depend only on your personal qualities, skills, and inner strength. And also on a coach, who we don't have."

"I don't need the coach," exclaimed Joe, driving along the pavilion and maneuvering like a pro. "Don't you see? I can do everything myself!"

The car jumped sharply up and turned on its side.

"Try 159 to 112, 117 to 585," Noi said. "You're the one with the car. Feel it and guide with your thoughts."

Joe did what he said and unexpectedly the car straightened out by itself.

"There!"

They drove up to the stands with cars hanging in the air and left the car. Noi walked from one booth to another, carefully reading the information.

"Here are the examples we can work with."

Joe stopped in front of a bright red-and-black car.

"Noi look!" he exclaimed. "All we need is to engrave the bird-lizard on the hood and it will be perfect!"

The mechanic approached him, and his eyes widened as he began to read the information board.

"Made in Bireya, from Orga black metal and Lyra crystals by

engineers from Puri and Kappa. That works," he nodded. "Noi will mod it so that it will fly better than any girza from Shilan."

"What?" asked Joe, not understanding. "Although this doesn't matter, I'll call it the Fire Lizard!"

The car descended onto the road. They sat inside and made several circles around the pavilion.

"I'm definitely taking it!" Joe exclaimed.

"Thanks for the purchase," said a voice that seemed to come from everywhere at once.

"What a day!" Joe yawned.

"Go to the hotel, Joe, and get some rest," Noi said. "Noi will take the Lizard to the workshop. A lot needs to be done."

"Thank you," said the racer, turning to the alien. "Really thank you, Noi. If it wasn't for you, I wouldn't be here."

Noi never looked prouder.

They both laughed, happy with what they had achieved so far. Not knowing what the universe prepared for them, they both looked forward to it as they felt that from now on, their life would be full of surprises.

Chapter 11
The Coach

◉

"How many stars are in the sky?"

"An infinite number."

"What about the planets?"

"Even more."

Joe was only five when his father put him in his Gurt racing car and they sped along the dusty road towards the horizon, strewn with small beads of stars.

"Will I ever be able to drive like you?"

"Of course you will." His father patted him on the head. "One day you will drive so fast that you will reach the stars, Joe. I promise."

But a loud sound broke this beautiful dream and forced Joe to open his eyes. It was the news again.

"Unknown Joe Dee Myers, from a planet that was previously thought to be outside of Orion districts, twelve hours ago received not only funding, but also full legitimization of his participation in the annual Orion Mega Race with incredible and one might even say surprising benefits. The Interstellar Committee has decided that if he wins, the planet will not only have a water supply, but also a permanent membership in the Orion's Maldoran District with access to all funds, programs, and activities."

"Yes, the boy is a hero. But what happens if he loses?" "Heroes don't lose, Lirta. Even when they lose."

"That's right, Pin. And to be honest, although I never bet, this year I will make a bet on him."

The announcers laughed and continued chatting. Ulit turned off the screen. He sat up in bed, looking at Joe's unusually pale face.

"What's happened?"

"They all believe in me."

"I do, too."

"What if I lose?" Joe got up and sat down again. "What if I don't come first?"

Ulit smiled sadly.

"You heard that heroes don't lose. And you, my little brother, are already a hero."

Joe walked over to the mirror, staring at himself.

"But still. Now too much depends on me. And you know how I hate that."

"Do not wind yourself up." Ulit went towards the door. "Just do what you love. You said yourself that racing is your life."

"I saw our father in a dream again, and again we went to the stars."

"I never see him."

"Imagine if he were here now. If he saw all this? What if now he is sitting somewhere in the universe, watching the news and thinking, 'This is my boy!'"

"He left us, Joe. He ran away," Ulit said sharply. "He left us and our planet when we needed him so much. Even if he is somewhere now, he is not here with us."

Not wanting to discuss it further, Ulit left.

Joe washed, dressed, and went out onto the flower-filled terrace, where Ulit and Noi were waiting for him. They sat at a table full of food. A light breeze was blowing, and ahead of them was a view of the ocean, boats bobbing on the waves and little houses on the mountain.

"It's not real, is it?" Joe held out his hand, and the mirage trembled.

"No, don't touch it."

But Joe touched it again. The mirage had changed and now they were sitting in the middle of a bustling city.

"Seventh star!"

Again, and now they were on the outskirts of a quiet, cozy alien village. He got tired of this game and sat down.

"Yesterday, I sat up until midnight trying to find us a coach," said Ulit. "All of them require a massive down payment and at least 20% of the winnings. We will give them 20%, but the upfront fee is a problem."

"Right," Noi agreed, "we can't afford it."

"But, while reading information about the importance of coaches, I came across the name of one of them, who not so long ago, forty years or so, was a legend."

Noi's eyes began to widen.

"His name is Pritmut Walsh from the planet Manzur."

"Oh, Pritmut!" Joe clapped his hands, and his eyes lit up. "He hasn't been in business for a long time though, has he?"

"Yes, but he produced six champions in a row. Nobody has been able to do this. Not a single coach. Producing one is already a stroke of luck, like winning the Mega Race lottery. But he produced six! And then he disappeared, not a single interview, not a single photo, not a word to reporters. Naturally, he is now one of the richest citizens in the universe and no longer interested in money, but I wondered: why did he disappear?"

Noi shook his head.

"That isn't an option. He killed him!"

"Killed who?" Joe asked, whilst deciding what to eat next.

"The seventh racer died without reaching the finish line," said Ulit, "not through his fault, of course."

"And whose fault?" Noi hesitated.

"Dozens of players die every year. They all know what they're getting into." Joe retorted.

"But he's a coach!"

"Yes, and he probably thought the same. Most likely, he blamed himself for this and disappeared," said Ulit.

"I didn't even know he was still alive," Joe laughed. "but what's in it for us?"

"I wrote to him on your behalf," said Ulit. "Told him about Melgera and about the water. And how I admire his success."

"And?"

Ulit was silent. Noi tried to keep his eyes still. And Joe ate everything that was on the table, looking at his brother every now and then.

"He answered," Ulit finally said after a deliberate pause.

"What??? Seventh Star!" Joe laughed like a child again, shaking his curls.

"Yes, he answered immediately, less than an hour after I wrote him. He said that he was aware of our situation and would take us without a down payment."

"But he killed him!" shouted Noi. "They say he is a sick psychopath!"
"He won't kill me." Joe kept eating.

"Maybe this time he just wants to redeem himself?" Ulit suggested. "At the cost of Joe's life?" Noi's indignation began to rise.

"One way or another, it's up to you," Ulit said raising his hands. "We can't find another coach."

"Noi is against it," said the alien, raising his voice. "Joe Dee Myers must live! He is the hero of the universe!"

"Come on, Noi," Joe giggled. "I won't live a thousand years like you anyway. I don't have long left. In comparison with you, I am a bug. So I agree."

"That means two against one," said Ulit.

"He's your brother!" Noi insisted. "You grew up together!"

"Yes, and as his brother, I think it's worth a try. One way or another, six players came to the finish line unharmed."

Noi mumbled something in an unknown language, and then got up and left.

"If I answer his letter now, he will be here within an hour."

"Go ahead." Joe shrugged and shoved another bite of cake into his mouth, then grabbed his stomach. "I think I ate too much."

Ulit drummed his fingers on the screen above his bracelet.

"Call him only Coach Pritmut. That's the accepted form of address. And remember that you wrote to him yourself. I had nothing to do with this."

"Understood."

"In all races, only the coach and the mechanic will be in touch with you, not counting other players, of course. The coach will see and read the maps. He will also dictate car settings for greater efficiency. Follow them or not, you choose. If the car breaks or gets damaged, you can teleport it to the workshop where Noi will repair it, but this, of course, delays you on the track."

"Sounds simple." Joe was yawning.

"If you take the fourth place, you won't get anything," Ulit continued. "The third one is quite a big cash prize. The second will provide you with a comfortable life on the best planets of the universe until the end of your
days. But first, is a jackpot, enough to buy and sell the future of entire planets. Only this can save Melgera."

"Got it. Got to be first." Joe nodded.

"Did you try to drive a race car yesterday?" Ulit asked cautiously. "Yes," the young man replied proudly. "I drive like a god!"

"Ok," Ulit exhaled with relief. "Because you have only a day before the first race."

"Don't worry, brother. Everything will be fine!"

Joe stood up, whistling his favorite song. "Well, shall we go?"
But Ulit remained seated.

"Now you are on your own, Joe," he said. "I did everything I could for you. And now I'll just sit here and watch what happens."

"Mmm," drawled Joe. "As you wish." He winked at Ulit and shouted: "Pavilion!"

The next moment, the sound of passing cars drowned out the space.

Joe appeared and looked around. There was no coach yet. "I wonder what he looks like?" Joe thought, looking at everyone present. But his thoughts instantly vanished as his gaze fell back on Elira Bright.

She stood all alone in the distance and looked at the track. She wore a short white dress, as if made of plastic, suited to her face and long flaxen hair, and high boots to complete the look.

A slight shiver ran through Joe's body, but he pulled himself together and walked towards her. The girl was so carried away that she did not notice how he approached.

"How boring is that?" he asked, standing next to her and looking where she was looking.

Elira shuddered and turned to him.

"How boring? Rewarding the winners of the Mega Race?" She smiled shyly and blushed slightly.

"On a ten-point scale from one to ten?" he insisted.

"5-6 probably," she answered reluctantly.

"I thought so," Joe shook his curls indignantly. "You dreamed of more!"

Elira looked into the distance. Joe followed her gaze and saw a cyborg staying there.

"Ah. Father doesn't allow it." Elira nodded.

"And what did you really dream about?"

"To become a spaceship pilot," the girl replied. The racer leaned to her ear and whispered,

"Then let's steal one of them right now and get away from all this boredom."

She laughed. He spread his arms and crossed them again on his chest.

"I drive really fast you know. They're not gonna get us. When it's too late, don't say I didn't offer it, okay?"

She kept laughing and he felt that he made the right first impression. "Joe Dee Myers," Elira said. "This year everyone is talking about you."
"And do you know who my coach is?"

The girl narrowed her eyes, reading information on the screen that appeared right in front of her.

"It can't be!"

"The legendary Pritmut Walsh himself!" Joe nodded.

"I can't believe he's back!" the girl exclaimed. "How did you manage to get him?"

"I can get anything I want," said Joe. "For example, tonight we will have dinner together."

Elira laughed.

"Maybe you should start with something simpler. Like winning the Mega Race, for example?"

"Oh, I get it," said Joe. "Dad doesn't allow dating either."

"What?" Elira was indignant. "I'm already sixteen. I can do whatever I want."

"Still, the influence of your father is obvious." "And who is your father?" she asked.

"A racer from the ghetto. He left my whole family when I was seven."
Elira's smile faded from her face.

"Oh, I'm so sorry. I didn't mean to…"

"Now you must dine with me, even if only out of pity," said Joe gravely.

Elira laughed again, but behind Joe came a low, harsh voice. "Racer Myers!"

Joe turned. A tall green alien with a bald, round head was

approaching him. In body and appearance, he looked like a slug, dressed in a long jacket. Its four thick, snail-tailed legs dragged across the floor as it moved forward, leaving a wet trail behind. The eyes were so big, bulging, even more than Noi's, and in its mouth, there was a long smoking pipe.

"Coach Pritmut," Elira murmured.

But he ignored her presence, glaring hard at Joe.

"What, kid, surprised? You thought everyone in the universe was bipedal like you, right?"

Joe, suddenly frightened, shook his head.

"Many change their appearance on purpose, adjust it to others, but I'm against it. You have to see things as they are, accept them as they are, and deal with it."

Joe held out a trembling hand to him, but the coach swam past and moved forward.

"See you tonight," Joe whispered to Elira and followed the alien.

"To be honest, I would never agree," the slug continued. "Especially because you're not worth a dime. This is obvious. But when I heard about water and about the planet, I almost shed tears. I don't think you came up with all this on your own. It's clear just by looking at you. But, oh boy, it is worth fighting for."

He stopped and flipped the pipe from the left corner of his lips to the right. Then he took out a flask and threw it to Joe.

"Take a sip. Don't be afraid. Just try."

Joe carefully took a sip. His face expression changed as he took another. It was delicious, terribly delicious.

"What is this?" he asked.

"Water, my boy, the best water. This is how it should taste. You've never tried it, have you?"

And Joe realized that he had never actually tasted pure water. For all the time he'd spent on Agarna, he drank only fruit juices and hot smoothies. Not to mention that all his life before, he had swallowed only wet dust on Melgera. And this, he couldn't even explain what it was like.

"Clean water from planet Fai," said Coach. "I order it by the truckload. But that's not the point. The point is that you're here for this."

He paused, watching Joe without taking his eyes off him. Then he lit his pipe and exhaled a cloud of smoke.

"I smoke spices on doctor's orders. Back pain and all that," he explained, as if Joe was asking. "Old age comes to everyone without exception. And when it comes, you look back and see what you did and what you lived for. You see all your victories and failures. And believe me, victories seem like a normal thing. You're not even proud of them. But mistakes... No, no. They gnaw at you, giving you no rest. And if you lose, kid, believe me, your old age will be worse than Vinaki's hell."

Joe did not know what he was referring to, but when he tried to imagine, for the first time in his life he was afraid for himself and his future; it felt so terrible that his knees trembled.

"And the water," the coach continued. "Billions will never try it." He yanked the flask out of Joe's hand.

"You little sprog," the coach barked almost angrily. "They are all looking at you! The whole universe turns on those channels to see how you, a frivolous little ghetto boy, accidentally got involved in the great games of existence!!"

"But it was not even me," mumbled Joe, justifying himself. "This was my brother Ulit. He…"

"Even now, you are not able to take even the smallest responsibility upon yourself, let alone deciding the planet's fate! I'll just tell you that the Universe conducts a dialogue with you personally, and with no one else. All the characters in your destiny are just scenery. But there's apparently no point in explaining anything to you, you worthless brat. Where is your car?"

"My car. Noi, is it ready?" the racer whispered in fear, turning away and pressing the button on his bracelet.

"Teleporting now," Noi answered briefly.

A car with a bird-lizard on the hood appeared in front of Pritmut. The slug examined it from all sides.

"Tolerable," he said. "Who modified it?"

"My mechanic Noi."

"Noi Hewitt," Pritmut inhaled deeply, while reading something in front of his eyes. "a talented Olerdean. Good."

Joe felt ashamed that he was not being praised and that he was maybe not so good after all.

"Here, take this." The coach put his hand into his pocket, took out a small device, and pricked Joe in the ear. He did it so fast that the racer jumped, not from pain, but from surprise.

"What is this?" Jumping back in fright, he yelled, "What have you done to me?"

"You're scared like a small girza," the Coach said contemptuously. "I installed a temporary implant in your ear. This is mandatory for all racers with coaches. It has 102 channels. One hundred racers, me, and Noi. Now, when you're on the road, you can switch them and contact any of the racers, as well as me or Noi, just by calling us by name in your mind."

"Fine, fine," Joe answered, still shaking, and got into the car. "Ride," the slug barked. "Ten times around the pavilion."

The racer sat down, started the car, and drove off. As soon as he moved ten meters away, he felt relieved. When the coach was around, reality seemed to electrify, and he felt fear and tension. But as he got further away...

"Myers!" Primut's command in his ears made his fear return in an instant.

"Yes, Coach Pritmut."

"I told you to go, not trudge like an ant." "That's what I'm doing!"

Joe continued around the track, every lap picking up speed, and then his car took off into the air.

"I'll tell you the settings. Let's see your reaction."

"Ok."

"75 to 132, 356 to 454, 95 to 117…"

Joe got nervous, but he pulled all his concentration together and quickly followed everything the coach said. The car roared and raced through the air at great speed up and down around the pillars of the stadium. Joe barely dodged when oncoming cars came across in his path.

Everyone on the ground looked up as Joe's car moved so fast it was almost impossible to catch it with an eye. Elira looked around. They couldn't take their eyes off him.

"Now it's more difficult," said the coach. "800 to 19, 378 to 745, 212 to 54 …"

The crowd only let out gasps of fear and relief as Joe dodged the obstacles.

"Pritmut Walsh is back!" someone shouted. "Is the driver the actual Joe Dee Myers?"

Joe hung in the air and the crowd cheered.

"Come back," said Pritmut. "Otherwise, they will start betting on you right now.

Joe slowly descended and parked in the corner, got out and ran to the coach. He breathed heavily, as if he had run several miles, and sweat was flowing from his face.

"How did I do?" he asked excitedly.

"You're a terrible racer," the coach concluded firmly.

Joe froze as if he had been doused in cold water and had a bucket put on his head. But the coach didn't care. He slowly moved forward, leaving its wet trail behind. Joe ran after him.

"Coach Pritmut, if I'm not good enough, can we practice again? We still have time!"

"It's not a matter of time, racer Myers. For some, it lasts forever. It's about what you do with it and what you fill it with. My time is valuable, and today I spent enough of it on you."

The coach left him behind, raising his hand when Joe wanted to say something.

Joe was angry. He tried so hard! But when he turned around, he saw that the whole stadium was looking at him. He shook his curls, and a champion smile immediately appeared on his face. And that familiar sweet feeling of universal admiration again washed over him like a warm wave.

Chapter 12

Caterpillar

However, not everyone who admires you wishes you success. Joe knew this from the looks some of the racers were giving him. He had not yet entered the racetrack, and they were already jealous of him, probably wishing him defeat. But this did not occupy his thoughts for long. He looked around the stadium in search of Elira, but she was nowhere to be found.

"Joe?" he heard and turned around.

Two young men stood in front of him. They were several years older than him. One was tall with a handsome face and neatly styled, gelled hair.

"Wut Hunger," he introduced himself and held out his hand. "A professional. Three times Dormart league champion, two Roland races, and fifteen local race wins. And you're a lucky one, right?"

He winked. The second shorter, stockier man was looking at Joe with undisguised interest.

"Binnie Juice, also a pro," he said. "I will not list my victories, but there are ten times more of them than Wut's."

"Don't lie," Wut laughed. "He lost to me at Dormart two years ago."

"Yeah," Joe said, shaking hands with them. "And I've won a couple of Gurt races."

"We all started somewhere," Wut nodded understandingly. "One way or another, you are already a legend. Although if you lose…" He hesitated and shook his head.

"Are you kidding? He got Pritmut Walsh," Binnie threw his arms up. "And how did you manage to get him?" Wut wondered.

Someone called out to them.

"Well, Joe," said Binnie. "It was nice meeting you. I'm here with my brother. His name is Harvey. He talks only about you. Come to the Caterpillar Bar in the evening if you want to relax before the first race. All participants of the Mega Race gather there."

"Thank you." Joe waved goodbye, and they left.

"Caterpillar Bar?" he thought. "An unfortunate name for a place of entertainment for racers."

He noticed that the pavilion was empty. Orientation meeting, Joe remembered.

He entered a spacious building. All one hundred racers of the stellar Mega Race gathered there. It was an indoor conservatory-like hall with high ceilings and stepped rows above which miniature racing cars circled, raced and overcame obstacles on holographic roads.

Racers sat or lay on soft chairs and watched the miniature show that played out over their heads. Joe saw Elira in the front row. She was talking to a young racer and smiling.

In an instant, Joe jumped over a few rows of seats and approached them.

"I don't want to interrupt you," he said politely to the young man. "But you have been requested to go to the registration room over there."

"Really? Ok."

The racer was surprised but he got up and headed in that direction anyway. Elira frowned in disbelief as Joe immediately sat down in his chair and, throwing his hands behind his head, smiled sweetly.

"Liar," said Elira. "Aren't you ashamed?"

"Not a bit." Joe shook his curls, and then took on a serious look. "So where did we get to last time? Spaceships, right? And where would you go if you had your own?"

Elira paused to think.

"To the world of the gods, of course. To Lagra." "Pfff. It doesn't exist! They say it is made up."

But Elira shook her head.

"It isn't. And today you will receive a proof of this."

Joe remembered the lessons of Universography, which he studied at school. There were four districts in Orion, Maldoran, Dormart, Grathea and X2, but many believed that there was a fifth called Lagra. No one has ever been there, but there were so many incredible legends about this place that it was called "the world of the gods."

"I see something," Joe said suddenly. He touched his temples with his fingers and closed his eyes. "Seventh Star! I see the future."

"And what's there?"

"There is...Lagra and the gods..."

"Mmm…," Elira closed her eyes and leant back, straightened herself in her chair as best she could, as if imagining it, too.

"Cities of indescribable beauty. Waterfalls of wonders, where any thought becomes real."

"Creatures that no one has ever seen in Orion." "Oh wait, I see something else in there," Joe said. "What?"

"It's me and you."

Elira laughed.

"Seriously! And we say to the gods, stop living only in our imagination! Appear now in the real world!"

"Silly." Elira lightly touched his shoulder. "You don't know anything about the real world."

"They don't exist! There are no gods! There is no Lagra." "Shhh." Elira put her finger to her lips.

The hall became quiet. Tewie, the coordinator, stepped onto the stage in front of them, and with him the cyborg that Joe had seen before. His iron body was covered in skin in several places, and half of his face glowed with azure light through the white plastic covering.

Tewie cleared his throat, getting ready to start his speech. A small microphone was hovering in the air in front of him.

"Greetings to all of you at the orientation meeting!" he said as loudly as he could. "All professionals!"

Half the room responded with joyful exclamations. "And all the lucky ones!"

The lucky ones rustled and whistled, and some stamped their feet and clapped.

"You did it! You have all achieved it! You have entered the top 100 chosen for the Interstellar Mega Race! The 100 favorites of both Orion and the universe itself."

The hall drowned in even louder noise.

"Let me introduce you to Mr. Judd Kraket Bright." He pointed to the cyborg. "President of the Interstellar Racing Committee."

"That's my father," Elira whispered, looking adoringly at him. "Who doesn't let you drive spaceships," Joe muttered.

For a moment, he imagined his father standing on that stage as well. What would he say?

"Judd, both professionals and lucky ones certainly have an idea about the Mega Race. But they cannot even imagine what awaits them tomorrow. So tell us what they don't know and what they should expect."

The Cyborg nodded.

"As you all know, for many centuries the Mega Races have been held with the support of the Interstellar Committee on its territory," he said and narrowed his eyes, scanning the hall. "This year, special thanks go to the head of the committee Ulka Lirit and members of the racing association, who find sponsors and continue to finance the improvement of this great event!"

The hall clapped.

"Judd, Judd," Tewie interrupted him. "Let me tell the guys right away that this year is special."

Judd nodded.

"That's right. This year we have prepared a surprise for you, worthy of making the name of each of you go down in history. The committee decided to take racing to the next level. I'll tell you honestly, we have been preparing for this for a very long time, and now the time has come."

He paused for a moment as a slight noise passed through the hall.

"Quit stalling, Judd." Tewie lightly pushed him in the shoulder, and the cyborg smiled. "Well, are you ready?" he asked loudly.

"Yes!" the hall answered in unison.

"The Interstellar Committee has come to an agreement with the head of the Play Like Gods corporation," said the cyborg. "All the obstacles on your race track will be organized by them. This is a whole new level! Neither we or you, can imagine what awaits us! These guys are in their business the best of the best! Their technology is classified and completely unheard of. Few of you know, but the Play Like Gods corporation was founded by a Lagrian, which means you have to play like gods, whether you like it or not!"

The hall got noisy, and Joe opened his eyes wide in surprise. "Seventh star!"

"I told you," Elira whispered. "Lagra exists."

Tewie raised his hand up, trying to calm the audience.

"But I'll get to the point and the rules." Judd's gaze slid over Elira, and then stopped and lingered on Joe, which made the young man feel uncomfortable. "The rules are simple. You will be driving through a huge and powerful hologram, which will be more real to you than anything you have encountered before. The races consist of three heats. The first one will eliminate fifty of you, so only half will get into the second one. And on the third, only twenty-five. But only the third race will matter and determine the winners!"

"And a little detail," added Tewie, "You can change cars only after the end of the current round! That means, you will need not only your skills, but also luck."

He spoke, but a semi-loud discussion of what had been said continued in the hall.

"Each race not only tests your speed but also consists of a series of increasingly difficult obstacles. You need to overcome everything you encounter and reach the finish line, which consists of two barriers. If you cross the first, you will automatically take second place. But only if you are first to cross the second barrier, you will take first place. The second barrier is your goal!"

He paused and looked around at the racers. Everyone in the room knew the rules. But the news of the upgrades arranged by the Lagrians seemed to shock everyone. When they had quietened down, Judd continued.

"You all know you are risking your lives. But this year this is reaching a new level too."

A miniature racing track appeared in front of the racers in the air.

"If before, obstacles on the road were dangerous, then this year, in addition to them, something truly terrible awaits you."

A cloud of darkness enveloped the mini track from all sides. Joe frowned.

"It is something that the Lagrians call 'darkness.' No one knows exactly what it is, but once you get there, you will die instantly. The darkness will be on the track and will tightly surround it from all sides. That is why you need to use all your driving skills to prevent this from happening."

"Judd," Tewie said. "Even I'm scared right now."

"Right," Judd agreed. "I do not envy you guys either, but all the pros and cons were carefully considered by the Interstellar Committee. An agreement with the head of the "Play Like Gods" corporation was signed for many years to come."

From the voices from the hall, Joe realized that not everyone was happy with this news. But he himself thought it was very exciting.

"And now…," Tewie shouted. "Something you all have been waiting for!"

There was a drum roll, and a short alien ran out onto the stage, and then jumped and stopped.

"Let me introduce you to Luuuuuudi Staaaaaar! The winner of the previous championship!"

The racers jumped up from their seats. They screamed so loudly that Elira covered her ears. Joe, on the other hand, tried his best to outshout the others. This went on for a very long time, as it was the actual Ludi Star, in the flesh.

Raising his arms above his head, the champion spun around, enjoying the moment. Finally, the crowd's hubbub subsided, and he, clasping his hands together gratefully, bowed and sat down on an invisible chair.

"I'll be honest and tell you right away; you won't like it!" he said seriously. "Forget all your previous races! Despair and pain await you ahead, and don't say that I didn't warn you! It only looks beautiful on screens. But in reality, everything is so much worse!"

"Ludi, you are the best!" Every now and then someone shouted from the hall, "you are my idol! Luuuuudi! Staaaaaar!"

"Remember, the main thing is to remain calm and concentrate! Also, listen to the coach. They have an instinct, they know what and how. It's difficult to navigate on the road, but the main thing...the main thing there is to find yourself. There you will meet a completely different version of yourself and see what it is worth, but I went through it, so you can too!"

"Ludi, we love you! Star, you are the best!" the crowd shouted.

"The empty-headed lucky ones," Joe heard a woman's voice say behind him. "Won't even let you listen. Why are they even allowed here? Everyone knows that they are only racing here to create a contrast to the pros."

Joe turned around and saw a beautiful thin alien with a sharp, almost evil look, orange hair in tight curls, and dainty hands with which she held up her chin.

"What are you looking at?" she asked rudely, "you won't even make it to the middle of the first round. I promise."

The racer made a face and stuck out his tongue at her, then chuckled and turned to Elira.

"That is Marva Tanto, a very serious opponent," she whispered. "Got seventh last year."

Ludi Star got up and, under another deafening roar of the hall, left the stage.

"Well," Tewie said. "I don't even have anything to add other than, go for it guys! Make history! What will you say to our racers for the road, Judd?"

"Remember why you are here," the cyborg said seriously. "Especially when you are on the track, and no matter what, never give up!"

The hall roared again. And when Judd and Tewie left the stage, everyone began to slowly disperse.

"Well?" Joe turned to Elira. "Shall we go to the Caterpillar Bar?" Elira shook her head.

"Anywhere but there."

"Come on, it'll be fun. The best racers will be there."

"I can't," she said firmly.

Joe sighed. He wanted to take her hand, stop her, talk more, but she was about to leave.

"You look more beautiful," he said suddenly. "More beautiful than who?"

"Than your poster on the wall in my room."

Elira smiled shyly and blushed, and then, wanting to hide it, turned away.

"See you later," she said. "And...be careful out there at the bar."

He watched her walk away, her light gait, her long flaxen hair, and for the first time in a long time, he felt lonely. He had to win the race, to win this opportunity just to be able to talk to her.

"Well, Joe, how was the orientation meeting?" The racer heard Ulit's voice coming from the bracelet on his arm.

"It was awesome," the young man laughed. "They complicated the track and the conditions."

"Hmm, do you think you can handle it?" "Are you kidding? I was born for this!"

"Great, then get back to the hotel as soon as possible."

"I can't. I need to go somewhere."

"Where?"

"It doesn't matter."

"Joe," Ulit's voice sounded stern. "You need to rest before the race."

"Don't be a bore, Ulit. You know me. I am the embodiment of self-control and discipline."

In response, there was only an incredulous sigh. Joe chuckled.

"All right, just come back as soon as possible. I was invited to the Golden Tribune. I wanted to tell you about it."

"What is it?"

"The meeting place of Orion's high society, where they watch the races. The elite, so to speak. I have no idea why they invited me there, though."

"C'mon. You are my big brother. All the doors in the universe should be open to you!"

"All right, Joe. Get back to the hotel soon and we'll talk. OK?" "No problem. Err, Ulit?"

"What?"

"Did you know that Lagra exists? I mean, really exists?"

"I did not believe it until today when I saw the news. It turns out that the "Play Like Gods" corporation belongs to a Lagrian. I still have doubts about this."

"Isn't it amazing?"

"I'm not sure it is. We don't know what to expect from them." "Expect my victory, brother. That's all!"

Joe laughed again and hung up the call. He felt like a king. He was talking to a girl he liked. He got the best coach there was, and now he was participating in the races arranged by the gods. With a light soul, he teleported to another location.

The Caterpillar Bar looked literally like a caterpillar. It was a long building with ten curves and multiple floors layered one on top of the other. Every now and then, it turned into a large neon-skinned caterpillar

that slowly crawled around the perimeter of the racer's town.

Aliens of all kinds flocked to the entrance. Among them were both the lucky ones and professionals. Many recognized Joe, waving to him, although he did not know anyone.

This place had such a captivating and dynamic feel to it that Joe decided he would be staying there for quite some time. He sat down at the counter and began to examine those present.

A robotic bartender in a colorful suit drove up to him. His smile was too wide, as if he was up to something but wasn't about to show his cards.

"Joe Dee Myers," he said, wiping the glass with a rag. "Welcome to the Caterpillar Bar. What will you drink?"

"Water, please."

"From what planet?" the bartender asked. "I have 815 kinds of water. All of the highest quality, of course."

From the moment Coach Pritmut treated him to it, Joe kept thinking of trying it again.

"From the planet Fai." He answered. "Great choice!"

A glass of water appeared in front of him. Joe drank it all at once. "More," he asked.

"So, they're telling the truth." The bartender smiled again, showing diamond teeth, "This is what you're here for."

Before Joe could answer, a young girl appeared in front of him.

She had long, black, braided hair and unusually large but very beautiful eyes with a clear look. She looked at him almost lovingly. This made the racer feel uncomfortable.

"Hi, Joe," she said. "I've been following your story since it hit the news."

"Really? Do we know each other?"

"Not yet. I'm Helga Lutto." She held out her hand to him. "You've hardly heard of me, but everyone here already knows you."

Joe's face lit up and he shook his unruly curls. He had heard it many times before, but each time was especially pleasant to him.

"Are you one of the lucky ones?" he asked.

"No, I'm a professional. But that doesn't mean anything, right? In Mega Race, everyone has an equal chance."

"It's not what I've heard. They say none of us will even make it to the second round."

"Not true. Mayer Ravter was a lucky one and in 17425 he was among the top ten champions of the third race."

"Well, that makes me feel better," Joe said, and took a sip of water. "Anyway, Joe, when I heard why you were here."

"Yes, yes. You thought, 'how noble!'"

"Exactly." The girl lowered her eyes, but then looked straight at him. "I believe that your victory will be a huge step for all the planets of the periphery of Orion! What you are doing is..."

But Joe didn't seem to be listening. He surveyed the hall and all present in it. Helga understood this and sighed.

"I just wanted to say I hope we'll be friends?" Joe looked at her.

"It's rare, of course. There are no friends in the race," she murmured. "But I wanted you to know..."

"Joe!"

She didn't have time to finish what she was saying when Wut, Binnie, and someone with a face completely covered in tattoos approached them.

"This is my brother, Harvey." Binnie introduced him and then lowered his voice to say, "Your number one fan."

Harvey had a cap and the T-shirt with Joe's face. Instead of a greeting, he pressed the button on his shoulder and a loud voice screamed, "Go, Joe!" which made everybody laugh for a long time.

Joe was sincerely glad to see them because they were real champions and next to them, he felt the same.

"And this," Joe turned, looking for the girl whose name he had already forgotten, but she disappeared.

"Come on, come with us," whispered Binnie. "Don't sit here with losers."

They pulled him deep inside the bar, which seemed to expand in all directions, and stopped at the table where several racers were already seated. Joe immediately recognized some of them. Only the best of the best were there.

"Only professionals here," Wut voiced his thoughts. "But don't be shy. We all know what you're worth!"

Joe couldn't hide his self-satisfied smile as they whistled and hooted when they saw him.

"Well, shall we bet?" Wut suggested as they sat down. The racers laughed.

"What?" Wut exclaimed. "Why can everyone bet on us, but we can't?"

"Yes, we should do it before anyone else," someone agreed.

"Then I'll bet on myself," said Binnie.

"And I, of course, on Joe," said Harvey.

"What will you drink?" the waitress asked.

They made their orders, and she turned to Joe.

"Water from Fai," he replied.

Everyone went silent for a moment. But Joe only ordered it because he was still entranced by how exceedingly good it was compared to what he had to put up with all his life.

"That's why," shouted Wut. "I bet 500 million Kharts on Joe right now!"

He made his bet. Everyone around laughed and applauded.

"And I think Mardo Keaton will win," Binnie said.

A screen appeared above the table, showing a racer. He was twice Joe's age. His car made incredible pirouettes, sweeping along the track. But what Joe was struck on most of all was his hard, focused look.

"He took second place in the Mega Race two years ago," Wut explained, "in addition 804 local victories in all four of Orion's districts. This is the level which we have yet to reach."

"They say he'd rather die than lose."

"Isn't he here now?" Joe asked.

The racers shook their heads.

"He never appears in public."

"Why would he need to? He already knows his worth."

They continued to talk about races and tracks, about those who invented them. The conversation kept returning to Lagra and the new conditions. Everyone was afraid of the darkness. No one knew what it was, where or how it appeared, or how it was teleported to the track. The more they talked, the more Joe felt he was exactly where he belonged. Here was everything he lived for, and he felt truly happy.

He ordered more and more water. At some point, Wut suggested that he drink water on a dare, and he agreed. Joe didn't remember what happened next. Only that it became too much fun for him. So much that it seemed to be going too far. They shouted and said different things, but he didn't even understand what he was saying.

At some point, Joe jumped up on the table and started shouting: "Do you want to know the truth? I'm not here for my planet and its water at all! To hell with it! I am a Gurt, and Gurts send absolutely everything to hell! And we are proud of it! The first thing I'll do when I win is get off of my planet and go to Lagra and that's it!"

He was answered with loud deafening applause. After that Joe fell unconscious.

Where was he? He did not remember and did not know, but it was absolutely pitch black. Perhaps this was that same darkness everyone was talking about. Maybe the Lagrians deliberately set it up so that he would not participate in the races? Joe didn't know, but he seemed to have already spent an eternity here. It was as if he was hanging in an infinitely dark universe in which the lights were turned off, and he could not move his arms or legs.

However, at some point, he heard a scream as if from far away. It was loud and shrill and somewhat familiar. But that wasn't what woke him up; it was the soft touch on his cheek and the smell. Such a nice soft scent.

Joe opened his eyes.

"Elira," he said.

"Yes, it's me," he heard in response. "Get up Joe. You're late for the race."

Joe abruptly opened his eyes. The girl stood over him and shook him by the shoulders.

"Raaaaacer Myyyyyers!!!!!!!!!!!" There was a deafening roar of the slug in his ears. "Why are you not racing?!!!!!!!!!!"

Joe instantly jumped to his feet. It couldn't be!

"You're late, Joe," Elira said regretfully. "They slipped 'riot-maker' and 'knock-out' in your drink and made a caterpillar out of you."

"What?" Joe couldn't understand anything, and he didn't want to believe what he heard.

"Dad says they choose a caterpillar every year. But I didn't think they would touch you."

"Joe, where are you?!" Ulit's voice was heard from the bracelet. "We have been looking for you all night!"

"Raaaaacer Myyyyyers!!!!!!!!!!!" rang in his ears again.

"Coach Pritmut," Joe murmured. "I don't know how it happened." He turned to Elira.

"What should I do to teleport to the starting line?"

"You can only get there on foot. If you hurry, you'll at least get on the track. The other racers started a minute ago."

Joe moved back, then turned and ran.

"Coach Pritmut," he shouted. "Tell me where I should go?" "Go?!" the coach roared. "You pathetic wimp!!!"

He then became silent.

"Coach Pritmut?! Coach Pritmut?!"

But there was no answer.

Joe ran through the racing town, not even knowing where the track was.

"Joe, Joe!" He heard and changed the channel. It was Noi. "Joe, where are you?"

"Just got out of the Caterpillar."

"Okay, it had crawled to the square... go to the middle of it and teleport to the pavilion. Then go three blocks to the right, then turn left, up the stairs to the fifth level when you get to the Crooked Path store…"

Joe ran as fast as he could.

"The well-known Joe Dee Myers not only was late for the start of the Interstellar Mega Race, but also said…" Every screen showed Joe standing on the table and screaming "I don't care about my planet" from the night before. The clip was on everywhere he looked.

As quickly as he could, he crossed the Racers' town and stopped at the gate. A small machine scanned him from head to toe.

"Racer Joe Dee Myers, welcome to the 754th Interstellar Mega Race." The gate slowly disappeared before his eyes.

"Come on, come on!" Joe exclaimed.

In front of him was a view of a sandy, endlessly wide road. Tewie, the coordinator, was slowly walking toward him.

"The bracelet," he demanded. "Extra communications during the races are prohibited."

Joe gave him the bracelet and looked around, there was no one there. Even on the horizon. Not a single racer!

"Where's my car, Noi?" he whispered.

"Every time you lose your car, you must call 'Lizard' and it will appear in front of you," the alien replied.

"Lizard," Joe shouted as loudly as he could.

The Fire Lizard materialized out of thin air. Joe got in quickly, turned on all the engines at once, and took off as fast as he could.

Chapter 13

Shifter

"Look at the Fire Lizard! Look how it rushes through the desert! Joe had a good time celebrating the start of the race the night before, but it looks like he's not going to give up!" the announcer said on the news.

Ulit turned off the screen, took off his glasses, and leaned back in his chair. He did not know for whom he was more worried, his brother or his planet. He stayed up all night looking for Joe, but what mattered most is that his brother had entered the race.

However, this morning Ulit realized that he had sent Joe to certain death. It wasn't that he didn't believe in his brother, but his desire to help Melgera made him forget what Joe would have to go through and that he could no longer help him. What if he lost? Terrifying pictures of Melgera's dehydration floated through his mind.

A shining port appeared in front of Ulit.

"Third Request for the Golden Tribune," he heard.

Ulit did not want to go there despite the importance of the event. What would he say to them now after Joe's stunt yesterday? However, he got up, washed his face with cold water, and stepped into the passage that appeared in front of him.

It was a spacious hall, where many aliens stood with glasses in their hands, celebrating the start of the race. Some of them were dressed stylishly and simply, while others were so colorful and pretentious that it seemed ridiculous.

Instead of walls, there were screens broadcasting the races. Translucent hologram scenes of the track and the cars occasionally left the screens and drove around the hall. They would also recreate the scenes of what was happening, forcing everyone to find themselves there, which delighted the guests.

"Ulit Dee Myers," said Tewie, who came up to him. "Greetings! I am the race coordinator," he was reminded. "My 35th race!"

"Pleased to see you," answered Ulit, looking around at the guests.

"These are the heads of planetary and space communities," Tewie explained in a whisper. "And the main sponsors, of course. Come on, they're waiting for you."

"Me?" Ulit adjusted his glasses. He felt out of place.

They approached a group of aliens and cyborgs, who immediately turned to face them.

"Ulit Dee Myers," Tewie breathed. "And this is Zelga Thelin, representative from Maldoran, Barver Zhar from Dormart, Nuan Kee from Grathea, and Marken Wu from X2. These respected gentlemen make sure that the participants from their districts receive fair treatment in the race."

Ulit forced a smile.

"We requested your presence here." Zelga winked.

"This is so interesting," said the fat-cheeked Nuan in a colorful suit, looking at him. "When I see aliens like you, I wonder who makes history? Heroes or those who stand behind them?"

The others nodded.

Joe's holographic figure materialized before them, shimmering with vibrant light. Raising his arms, he greeted everyone in the room with infectious enthusiasm.

"It seems the boy doesn't care about his planet and its problems, but you..."

"I spent a lot of effort trying to prove that Melgera belongs to the Maldoran district of Orion, and Joe supports me in this."

The next moment, holographic Joe was standing on the table, shouting, "I don't care about my planet," and Ulit felt ashamed.

"Hardly," replied the tall Barver with four arms. "However, you rolled the dice and played luck with the universe itself."

"And now we are trying to figure out which of you is the shifter?" said Marken, a tall cyborg. "You see, we have our own bets."

"Shifter?"

"Yes, this is someone with a strong energy field," explained Zelga, a plump, beautiful alien. "So strong that it is capable of spinning energy of planetary proportions, changing the history of entire constellations, if not more."

"The intention of shifters is so strong that they subjugate reality and shape it according to their goals."

"Ahh." Ulit held out and adjusted his glasses. "And you think this is one of us?"

"The fact that it is one of you is already obvious," she continued. "Now we are trying to understand who."

The politicians turned to the screens, where a close-up of Joe in the

Fire Lizard was racing towards them.

Joe pressed on the driving pedal as hard as he could and rushed forward. The coach did not answer his call, and only Noi kept cheering him on with a confident "Go, Joe!" or "You can do it!". But Joe did not know at all where to go because the coach had all the maps.

"It seems the caterpillar has become a butterfly!" he heard Binnie's sly voice say as he switched to the racers' channel.

"I hope you're not offended, Joe," said Wut, laughing. "You understand that it was just a friendly joke."

But Joe was as angry as he had ever been in his life, so he just remained silent.

"Oh, our hero is still offended," Harvey mockingly whined, and then added seriously, "I want you to know, Joe. I don't care about you as much as you care about your planet!"

That was enough. Joe switched the channel back to Noi. "Where should I go?"

"Noi has no idea, Joe," he replied regretfully. "But he warned you that Pritmut was no good."

At that moment, Joe again felt the urgent request to the racers' channel and switched.

"Joe." He heard a thin female voice that seemed familiar to him. "Helga?"

"Yes, it's me. I wanted to ask how are you? The coach said that you managed to start."

"I did," Joe replied. "But I don't know where to go." He was ashamed to admit it.

"Oh," Helga replied. "Where are you?"

"It's like a sandy road."

"Ah, the eternal road. To enter the obstacle course, you need to drive away from the sun."

Joe stopped the car abruptly. He only now realized that the sun was blinding his view. He turned around and drove in the opposite direction.

"Coach Pritmut," he called. "Coach Pritmut, I'm heading out to the obstacle course!"

But Pritmut was silent, and Joe thought that perhaps the slug was yelling so loudly that he broke the channel and now he would definitely not be able to contact him.

Suddenly a long, massive tentacle hit the road and broke it in two. Joe braked hard and took to the air in a lightning-fast maneuver. There, from above, he saw a giant octopus. Its terrifying tentacles slammed the ground, leaving gaping black cracks, and then flew up, trying to catch Joe.

The racer barely managed to dodge his blows, but the worst thing was that no matter how hard he tried, he could not move forward, and below on the ground, there were several racing cars broken into pieces.

As time passed, Joe's attention weakened, and his strength was exhausted, but the octopus continued to twist its tentacles so furiously that even the slightest mistake could cost Joe his life. At some point, it caught him. Joe managed to break free, but he had no strength to move forwards. He realized that this was the end and let go of the steering wheel.

"To hell with all of it!" he thought, "I'm really worth nothing!"

His car hovered in the air and then began to slowly fall.

"78 to 784, 158 to 462, 874 to 184, 13 to 222," Joe heard.

It was Coach Pritmut! Joe immediately grabbed the steering wheel and followed his instructions, barely dodging the blow of a huge tentacle.

Pritmut dictated the settings so fast that Joe could barely keep up with what he said. But after a few minutes, he broke out of the vicious circle, and the octopus was left behind.

"Coach Pritmut!" joyfully exclaimed Joe, "I'm so glad to hear you!"

But the coach remained silent. Joe got down to the ground and stopped the car. He couldn't catch his breath. His hands were trembling. He felt terribly tired, and this was only the first obstacle. He definitely didn't expect this. The sun was scorching mercilessly, and Joe realized he didn't have a drop of water.

"Where to now, Coach Pritmut?" he asked. "Tell me, where should I go?"

"What if I don't tell you?" the slug replied angrily. "What if you die here because you failed me and everyone else?"

Joe looked around. The desert was endless.

"OK! Let it be so. I'm not what you expected. I understand! But now we're tied, right? If I lose or die it will be on your conscience alone."

The coach was silent.

"How did you say it? It will torture you until your death, worse than some kind of hell!"

Pritmut was silent for a long time, and it seemed to Joe that he would never return. The sun was getting hotter and hotter, and Joe realized that he would not last long.

"If it wasn't for me, you'll be the last to finish," Coach said suddenly.

"Agree," shrugged Joe and lay down on the seat.

"I want you to say, 'Coach Pritmut, without you, I'll come last.'"

"Ok," said Joe. "Coach Pritmut, without you, I'll come last."

"Louder."

"Coach Pritmut, without you, I'll come last!" Joe screamed as loud as he could.

The coach exhaled spice smoke in his ears.

"Start the engines, you waste of space," said Pritmut. "749 to 117, 574 to 983."

Joe got into the car and followed his instructions.

In the Golden Tribune, the guests were reclining on the couches. They followed the drivers and discussed the most dangerous moments on their track. Ulit watched Joe with a pounding heart.

"He seems like a bright boy." Nuan was clapping his hands watching Joe breaking out of the octopus's clutches. "But if it weren't for the coach, he wouldn't have made it."

"Don't belittle his merits," said Marken. "We all know that coaches win races, but if they were behind the wheel, none of them would cope with even the smallest obstacle."

"True," Barver agreed. "Usually the most successful duo wins."

"How did you manage to get Pritmut Walsh anyway?" asked Zelga, turning to Ulit.

"He just agreed." Ulit shrugged. "Things like that don't just happen."

Ulit watched the other guests. They made bets, not only for money, but for decisions on personal disputes, major contracts, and the fate of entire peoples and planets. And they noisily discussed everything that happened to the racers.

"250 billion that Mardo Keaton will be in the top five in the first round," Zelga said, watching the racer weave through the obstacles.

"Bet accepted," said a voice from nowhere.

She sipped her cocktail nonchalantly. Ulit's got goosebumps when he imagined how much money it was.

"570 billion for Binnie and Harvey," Barver said, cracking nuts. "And Nuan, I will give you any three political prisoners if your Lutto wins this round, and you will give me mine if Tanto does."

"Agreed, but I choose the captives."

"Contract 5817, if Joe makes it to the second round," Marken said, looking at Barver. "In exchange for whatever you want."

"No." He shook his head. "You know Ulka will kill me for such bets."
"Since when do you care?"

Barver leaned back in his chair, staring up at the ceiling, then turned to Marken.

"Fine, but if he enters the top ten in the second round, the contract is mine!"

"Deal."

He winked at Ulit, who thought about how easy it was to decide fates here.

Joe was racing forward through the desert when the track changed and turned into a series of tall rocks intertwined and twisted into various formations up to the sky.

The racer could barely keep up with Pritmut's torrent of commands. Maneuvering between them lasted for what seemed like an hour, when suddenly he began to see racing cars on both sides of him. He whistled with joy as he overtook them.

"The speed is phenomenal! What did you stuff the Lizard with, Noi?" he asked.

"With all the best," the alien answered with pride.

Something hit the car sideways with force, knocking him off the track. Then again. Joe looked out the window.

"We have guests!"

On both sides of the car, he saw large birds with mouths full of teeth. "Aren't these actual bird-lizards?" Joe exclaimed.

"No, these are Roovies from the planet Navan."

Dangerous creatures," said Pritmut.

The racer barely dodged them, and the birds kept clicking their beaks, almost keeping up with the car. One of them hit the windshield and made a hole in it. Small cracks fanned out over the glass.

"I can't see anything, Coach," shouted Joe, not knowing where he was going.

"100 to 54, 500 to 772, 895 to 337, 142 to 456," Pritmut jabbered.

But Joe couldn't manage and lost control. The Lizard flew into a dry tree at full speed and got caught in it.

The desert landscape turned into high cliffs hanging over the raging ocean, on the edge of which was the tree with Joe's car hanging on it.

The tree made a menacing creak.

"Coach Pritmut, I'm stuck!"

"Is the car good for underwater?"

"Noi didn't make it," Noi replied, almost crying. The tree tilted and broke in half.

"Teleport the car to the workshop now," yelled the slug. "Noi, get the Lizard."

The Lizard disappeared and Joe, along with the broken tree, flew down with a desperate cry.

He fell into the water and began sinking to the bottom. He could see someone's racing car laying upside down on the sea bed. With all his strength, he began to swim up, but when a whirlpool dragged him down with force, Joe began to struggle.

"Relax, don't move your arms and legs, or you'll die," the coach's voice sounded in his ears.

Joe did as he was told. After a moment, the whirlpool's funnel that was sucking him down stopped spinning and dissolved.

"Now move up!" the coach commanded.

Joe's chest was ready to explode, as he desperately wanted air, but he summoned up all his will and after half a minute, he finally reached the surface.

"Can you actually swim?" the coach asked as Joe gasped for air. "Remember there is no water on my planet, Coach," Joe said. "Too bad. You are 300 meters away from the shore."

Joe intuitively moved his legs and arms, and little by little, figured out what he had to do.

"I think I'm good at it!" he exclaimed. "Faster!" the coach yelled.

But Joe stopped. Right in front of him, a big monster without eyes jumped out of the water and plunged back in.

"These are Kewai from the planet Gurzak," Pritmut explained. "They are toothless and blind, but one of them can swallow you whole and not even choke."

Joe felt a wave of fear running though his body, but he began to swim as fast as he could.

"Big one on the left," the coach said. The racer veered to the right. "Freeze!"

The monster vanished.

A hundred meters further on and another kewai's tail touched his leg. Another hundred more and Joe dodged two at once as they summersaulted back into the water.

Just when the land became tantalizingly within reach, another one emerged from the water and flew at Joe, with its mouth wide open. The racer dived and began to swim down to avoid the creature.

"To the right! Right!" shouted Pritmut.

But the kewai grabbed Joe by the leg and pulled him along. Joe knew he had not inhaled enough air and began to lose consciousness.

"Racer Myyyyyers!" yelled coach, "Myyyyyers!"

The shouting made the racer open his eyes and confront the beast. With all his strength, he pushed off from it with his free leg and rose to the surface. He coughed until the coach's screams grew loud enough to drown out all other sounds.

"Move, Myers, move!"

Land was nearby, and the young man swam towards it with the remaining strength he had left. Finally, he reached the shore and lay down on the sand exhausted. He wished he could stay there for at least a few hours. But the scream in his ears didn't let him rest.

"Get up, now! You're wasting time, you little snot!"

The Lizard appeared nearby. The windshield was like new. Joe opened the windows and got off the ground, enjoying the light breeze and the soft light of the sun.

"Uhhh," he shouted. "Coach Pritmut, it's not that bad here! I even like it!"

"You're still behind the majority, you smug fool," the coach reminded him.

"So, I'm not the last?" Joe asked, pulling racing goggles over his eyes. "Coach Pritmut, you definitely know how to cheer me up!"

He slammed on the motion pedals with full force and flew forward as fast as he could.

The landscape changed and Joe flew onto a clear section. With a joyful cry, he overtook two racing cars. But they pressed on and caught up with him again. When Joe swerved to the right, they followed him, and when he went to the left, and both cars squeezed him so that he could not turn, and a dead end was approaching.

"All levers down, 340 to 215," commanded Pritmut.

The car dived down, did a few somersaults in the air and finally levelled off. The racer broke free from their grip. One of the cars behind him hit the obstacle. Joe managed to jump over it and carry on.

"That's how it's done!"

He rushed forward, overcoming the obstacles that continued to appear in front of him for about half an hour, when suddenly the landscape changed again; a dense wall of wind and sand rushed towards the racer.

"The deserts of Rui," said Pritmut. "Here the main thing is not to be afraid."

And he began to dictate the settings. The Lizard was flailing from side to side with such force that everything was merging before Joe's eyes, and sand was blasting against the windshield.

The racer did everything the coach told him and the sand gradually disappeared. The Lizard hovered in the air and moved from side to side, not responding to his control.

Trying to stay in one place, Joe checked all the engines, sliders, and levers. But no matter how hard he tried; he could not move forward. Joe looked out of the window.

"Seventh star!"

"Hush" the coach whispered. "You were caught by a fisherman monster from the planet Iji."

Joe's car hung on a huge fishing rod, which was held in the hands of a one-eyed monster. It had an odd shaped head and a round mouth filled with frightening teeth. He had an evil but silly expression, and would occasionally look pleased with all the cars that he had caught with his rods.

"How bad is it?" Joe asked as he let go of the steering wheel.

"Wait," said the coach "I'm reading information about them. Yes. Despite the frightening appearance, they have the intelligence of a baby, and they love everything bright and noisy."

"How can this help us?"

"It won't. Get out of the car and climb up the rope."

"Are there other options?" Joe asked, looking down. The ground was way too far.

"Do not argue with me!"

Joe had no choice but to open the door and climb up. The car tilted and he almost fell.

"Coach Pritmut, I don't think I can!" he yelled. "You can or I'm not Coach Pritmut!"

Joe thought that it was a compelling argument. Gathering all the strength that he had, he grabbed the rope, held it with his feet and climbed up. He looked down, the Lizard disappeared, and the head of the giant was getting closer.

"Try not to attract his attention. You need to get out on a flat surface as soon as possible."

Joe's face twisted when he smelled the terrible stench emanating from the Cyclops. He reached the top of the rod and wrapping his arms around it, slid down the stick and fell on the giant's wrist.

"Try to step carefully so that he does not feel your presence."

Joe tried, but the smell was so awful that he could not stand it and sneezed. The monster raised his hand to his eye and looked at the racer with interest.

"You must distract him, or he'll shake you off!"

"Where there is no horizon and the bottom is not seen, the Seventh Star shines, clear and bright, like a dream..." Joe sang as loudly as he could as he danced on monster's arm.

The cyclops opened its mouth, but then laughed so loudly that Joe covered his ears with his hands and continued to sing anyway. The monster raised its other hand and was about to slap the racer.

"Run," commanded Pritmut.

Joe ran up the cyclops's arm, dodging the blows.

"Lizard!" he shouted and jumped into the car that appeared in front of him.

He narrowly missed driving straight into the giant's toothy mouth but regained control and rejoined the race.

Barely tearing himself away from the screen, Ulit looked around the Golden Tribune.

"Everyone knows that more than half of the racers die or get seriously injured in the race," Marken said, sipping his cocktail.

"Yet billions want to participate," Nuan added.

"And they easily destroy rivals, without any remorse," said Barver. "I like it so much!"

"Another detail about shifters," Zelga whispered, looking at Ulit. "They don't care about others. They can sacrifice anything and anyone for their goals."

Ulit swallowed nervously and the feeling of guilt that he experienced that morning returned to him. He turned away, looking around the room.

All those present were rooting for their idols. Joe's name was heard now and again. He walked around the hall and noticed that two unknown aliens were looking at him.

"Who are they?" he asked Tewie.

"These are the sponsors," the coordinator answered. "Rod Hunger and Lear Juice."

"Their sons race, don't they?"

"They do," Tewie whispered. "Also, they are strongly against the entry of small border planets into the Orion districts. That's why they are a special danger to Joe."

Ulit looked at the sponsors. They raised their glasses.

"I can't reveal all the secrets," continued Tewie. "You will see everything for yourself. But let me show you something interesting."

He winked at him and put a small sticker on Ulit's wrist.

As soon as he did so, Ulit appeared in the Fire Lizard right next to Joe. This happened so suddenly that even his glasses fell off. The simulation of reality was near perfect.

"Joe," Ulit called, but his brother neither heard nor saw him.

Ulit was so scared he couldn't bring himself to look ahead. The speed at which they were rushing seemed to make everything melt and blur. The reaction needed to stay on the track had to be perfect. After a few seconds of being in the car Ulit realized that he couldn't bear it any longer and ripped the sticker off.

"Which one of us is a shifter?!" he thought. "Certainly not me!"

Joe continued to move forward, completely unaware that his brother had been in the car with him.

"Be careful. There is a series of unexpected obstacles ahead," Pritmut warned.

The landscape changed. Joe was rushing through empty space, but in front of him obstacles would still appear out of nowhere. These were parts of buildings, cars, living beings, all kind of things. The racer remembered the meerkat at the Gurt stadium. Now, he wouldn't let that kind of thing confuse him.

"Focus, Joe! Pay attention!" the coach said between instructions.

"This is the first time you've called me by name, Coach. I'm deeply touched," said the racer while he was having to ascend and descend again and again.

"Don't think that you and I will ever become friends," Pritmut replied.

"I can't even imagine that," Joe answered. "Besides, I don't know anything about friends."

"I know they made a caterpillar out of you," the coach said suddenly. "And yet you abandoned me!"

Pritmut was silent.

"Don't worry, I'm not offended!" said Joe.

"We choose the society that holds us back or pushes us forward. And this choice shapes our destiny. I thought you were a loser, Myers, but maybe you're not."

"That's so nice to hear!"

Joe laughed as he dodged the obstacles and overtook two competitors. Suddenly, clouds of something impenetrably dark began to appear in the air from all sides.

"Is that what I'm thinking?" Joe asked as he maneuvered between them.

"Yes," the coach answered. "That's the darkness. They say it's dangerous to even look at it."

The impenetrable clouds, black as an abyss, swirled with patterns and seemed to fascinate the racer. Joe stared and almost drove into one of them.

"Concentrate, Myers," barked Pritmut. "545 to 647, 237 to 412, 594 to 762…"

As he continued to dictate the settings Joe moved forward fast, reality transformed into a curving tunnel through which several other racers were rushing. One hit Joe in the side with all its force but Joe responded in kind, nudging him off the track.

Another racer turned sharply and blocked his path, but Joe jumped up and over it, hitting the next one in line off its course. In the next moment, a few cars were competing with his speed, racing neck and neck.

"All engines full on, Myers. You have to outrun them. Now the only thing that matters here is speed!" shouted Pritmut so loud that Joe, out of fear, found that he had left a few cars behind.

Joe felt the rush, the speed, and the adrenaline that drove him forward. He used to do this for no particular reason other than crossing the finish line first and that was it. He liked being first, nothing else. But now so much depended on his victory. He fully realized it at that moment.

All of a sudden, he drove through a radiant wall of light.

"Do not slow down," said Pritmut. "You've passed the first barrier! But when I say stop, you must stop. Do you hear?"

"Yes, sir," Joe answered carelessly.

He continued to rush forward and overtook three more cars, when suddenly Pritmut shouted as loudly as he could:

"Stop, Myers!"

It took a moment for Joe to realize but the racer immediately pressed all the brakes at once. A huge black wall appeared ahead of him, and he continued heading straight at it.

"Brake!"

Joe turned the car sharply. It did a somersault, crossed a small, barely visible line in the road, and parked just passed it.

"Congratulations. You've crossed the second barrier," said the coach. But Joe ran out of the car and froze, staring at the black wall.

"What is this?" he asked in confusion.

The coach remained silent. It was darkness, vast, impenetrable, and bewitching. There seemed to be no hint of light in it or anything that would give an indication of life.

"Go back to the pavilion, Myers." The coach exhaled spice smoke in his ears. "You did pretty well today."

But Joe was so mesmerized that he forgot everything. He even forgot that he was at the Mega Race and was a participant in it. He didn't even care where he was.

Barely taking his eyes off the black wall, he entered the small door. There were no thoughts in his head. He walked through the tunnel. Another racer followed him. They passed through the port and...

The noise was so deafening that Joe had to cover his ears. Everyone in the pavilion shouted and the audience on the screens screamed nonstop. Above all the din, the announcer pronounced the names of those who entered the top fifty. It seemed that all the attention of the universe was centered here.

Ulit met Joe with his usual fatherly smile and hugged him tight. "Did I make it?" Joe asked, finally coming to his senses.

"You are in 49th place," Ulit answered.

"Seventh star! It means I'm in the second round! Yes!" Joe jumped up and down, raising his hands and shaking his curls.

Drones flew around, trying to capture the reaction of the participants.

"I'm doing this for the sake of my planet, just for you to know," Joe said loudly, making a face at them, and then laughed like a child.

"Let's go," said Ulit. "A press conference is waiting for you, and then you need to rest."

 Joe continued waving at the crowd and smiling as widely as he could. How he loved those moments, when everyone adores you because you can do something no one else can, and you do it well.

"They told me something interesting today at the Golden Tribune," Ulit shouted into his ear.

"What?" Joe asked, trying to be heard above the noise. "That you are a shifter."

"Who?"

"You'll never believe..."

Joe stepped on a pedestal where he was asked questions, filmed, and photographed. At that moment, he felt as if he had merged with the universe, it was such a blissful moment.

Chapter 14

Friends of the Star Baron

Joe was in a deep sleep, but even there he could hear the stadium chanting his name. Somewhere in the audience, he noticed his father. For some reason he didn't jump for joy like the others. He just looked at him with a sad face. When Joe moved towards him, he disappeared into the crowd, which grabbed the racer in their arms and crowd-surfed him forward.

"Joe!" a voice said, insistent.

The young man opened his eyes. Ulit was standing over him. "The second press conference is waiting for you."

Joe rubbed his sleepy eyes and turned on the news screen.

"All the eyes of the universe today are on Mardo Keaton, the finalist of the first qualifying round of the Mega Race, as well as on the other finalists, among which are the already well-known Wut Hunger, Marva Tanto, and..." the announcer continued to list the names.

Joe jumped up and sat up in bed. He waited for his name to be spoken. But the fact that he was not among the first painfully pricked his pride.

"The Juice brothers did not even reach the twentieth place. If not for the breakdown of the car, they would have been among the first," the announcer continued.

Joe giggled. He was so pleased to hear that.

"However, they finished in the top fifty, as did the infamous Joe Dee Myers, who was late to the race but finished 49th! He may not be doing it for the sake of his planet, as he promised, but his racing prowess was enough to be one of only five lucky ones to make it to the second round!"

"49th place. Seventh Star." Joe covered his head with a pillow.

"In my opinion, this is excellent," Ulit encouraged him. "Considering that you started twelve minutes later than the others."

"Mardo! Mardo! Mardo! Keeeeeeton!" the crowds chanted. Ulit switched the screen to Melgera's local channel.

"Better watch this."

Crowds of Melgerians, both Gurts and Orans, chanted his name. "Joe! Joe! Joe! Deee! Deee! Deeee! Myyyyyeeers!"

There, on his planet, he was a hero, despite yesterday's scandal.

Joe went towards the mirror. He looked at the bird-lizard tattoo on his arm. Gurts, Orans, and Melgera were so far away. Now he suddenly realized that their love was not enough. He wanted more - to be known on every planet of Orion. He wanted his name to be screamed out by the universe itself.

"Joe," the racer heard Noi's sad voice in his ears, "Noi let you down." "What? What are you talking about?"

"Noi let Joe Dee Meyers down and because of him he came 49th."

"Not at all, Noi. You did a great job! The car is just perfect. Rushes through the air like lightning!"

"Noi didn't set it up for sub aqua mode," the mechanic said in a voice that sounded tired and trembling.

"Why don't you rest, Noi? You did great!"

"Noi won't leave the workshop until Joe Dee Myers takes first place in the Mega Race!"

Joe went out onto the terrace and turned to the rain. Large drops drummed on the umbrella that covered the table. He watched them fall into the ocean and cause ripples through the gentle waves.

"I ordered your favorite water from Fai," Ulit said, coming up to him with a decanter.

"I hope it doesn't have knock-out or trouble-maker in it," Joe asked cautiously.

They ate a selection of dishes for breakfast that were quite unknown to them, but both agreed that their taste was out of this world.

Joe looked unusually serious.

"What are you thinking about?" Ulit asked, watching his brother.

"About this," said Joe, spreading his arms. "About all this. Why aren't we a part of the Orion?"

"Ah," Ulit drawled. "That's what I've been fighting for the last ten years."

Joe ruffled his hair and propped his cheek with his hands.

"What if I lose?" he asked. "What if I don't make it to the third round?"

"I don't think you need to worry about that," said Ulit. "One thing I know for sure: on the road you are always in your element, no matter the reason you are there."

"But I'm afraid not only for our planet, brother, but for myself," Joe shook his head. "No matter how selfish it sounds, I'm thinking, what will happen to me? Without these races, love of the crowds, without the attention of the universe, my life will have no meaning."

"It will, Joe."

"Why didn't you give up after our father left?" Joe asked suddenly. "What made you come out of the Gurt slums?"

"Some kind of feeling," Ulit replied. He took off his glasses, wiping off raindrops, "Sort of like a call to move forward."

"To move forward," Joe repeated. "Seventh Star!"

He didn't have time to reflect on that, as before the shining port appeared right next to them.

"Request for the second Press Conference," a voice said softly.

"We have to go." Ulit threw a racing jacket to his brother.

At the press conference, all eyes were on Mardo Keaton's table, who took first place, as well as Wut Hunger and Marva Tanto, who came second and third.

Listening to the answers to the questions they were being asked, Joe felt something that he had almost never experienced before. He envied them. He should have been sitting there.

At some point, his eyes met with Helga Lutto, who was sitting at the second table. That meant she was in the second ten. She smiled and waved at him.

The Juice brothers, who were sitting at the third table, kept throwing mocking glances at him.

"A question for Joe Dee Myers," said one of the reporters.

Joe winced briefly, but his signature champion smile quickly took its place.

"You performed well on the track and now you are among the five lucky ones who advanced to the second round. What is it like to be the lucky one among the professionals?"

"I feel truly lucky."

Those present in the hall laughed.

"They say that lucky ones win thanks not to their own merits, but due to luck. What do you think?"

"I don't think. I race, and I win."

"Pfft. And this comes from the 49th placed racer." Binnie laughed wickedly.

But Joe ignored him and continued to smile.

"How would you comment on your behavior on the eve of the race?"
"I drank too much water."

The hall laughed again.

"And yet there are doubts that you will spend the winnings on what you promised."

"Look," said Joe. "I really said too much. But words don't mean anything. My actions are much more important. I admit, I did not think about my planet's problems before; I was too irresponsible. I am who I am. But now I'm sitting in this room. Is it because of my efforts or luck? I don't know! I only know that a lot depends on me. That my winning or losing is a step forward or backward for the whole planet, and for all the planets of the periphery of Orion. So, no matter what I say, the only thing that counts is whether I come first in the third race or not, right?"

Ulit, who was sitting in the hall, nodded approvingly, as did many reporters. They continued to ask questions, but Joe looked at Elira, who was sitting next to her father. He was in 49th place, but that made him a little closer to her than before.

As he was about to leave the hall, the Juice brothers blocked his way.

"The caterpillar may have become a butterfly, but it is easy to squash," Harvey said through clenched teeth.

"Take it easy, guys," said Joe. "In this race I gave you a head start, but in the second, if you behave badly, this will not happen again."

"Don't listen to them, Joe," said Wut, who came up and held out his hand. "We had a little fight, but we're still friends, right?"

But Joe didn't shake his hand.

"That's all right," Wut said and patted him on the shoulder. When the brothers moved away, he whispered, "If I were you, I would add the 25XC function to the car. This is to forget old quarrels. Don't thank me."

He winked at the young man, then glanced at Elira approaching them, and left.

"Noi," Joe called. "Yes, Joe."

"Is there a 25XC function in my car?"

"By tomorrow morning it will be there," the mechanic replied. Joe's face lit up as Elira approached him.

"You saved me there yesterday morning. How can I thank you?"

"Don't worry," the girl said. "If there's one thing I love about my job, it's the moments when I give real help."

She blushed a little, and Joe, noticing it, smiled. "What about the dinner you promised me?"

"I did not promise you anything!"

"No, I think I remember. You said, 'Listen, Joe, if you don't die out there on the track, let's have dinner at...'"

"The Caterpillar?" Elira laughed.

"No, not there! This time you'll have to rescue me from some other bar."

"How about Friends of the Star Baron? All the finalists will gather there soon. And I will be there, too."

"Why was it named that?" Joe asked suspiciously. "I already realized that all the places in the racing town have some kind of catch."

"This one doesn't," said Elira. "There's just a legend that it was founded by the Star Baron himself."

Joe did not even know who he was, but he was already sure that he would definitely be there.

Someone called to Elira, so she waved goodbye to Joe and left, and he remained watching her talking to the race organizers in the distance for a long time.

"Your little speech there was great," said Ulit, who came up to him. "even I could not have written it better."

"You told me yesterday that I'm...what was it...a shifter?" reminded Joe. "So it's time to get down to business, change the fate of planets and constellations, isn't it?"

He paused but then stared into his brother's eyes.

"I know you don't approve," he said carefully. "But I'm going to a party. All finalists will be there. It might be useful for me. I can ask them a few things."

Ulit smiled with his usual fatherly smile.

"Only if you promise to be careful, Joe. You know too many people want you to fail."

Joe nodded and waived as he watched the drones capturing him from afar. Saying goodbye to Ulit, he left the pavilion and went to the town.

What a pleasure it was to walk around the planet Agarna and be a racer who made it through to the second round of the Mega Race!

Joe wandered the streets looking for the bar Elira was talking about and saw a small market. He walked there and examined all kinds of goods from all over the universe when a blue-skinned alien approached him.

"How can I help you?" he asked.

"I'm looking for a gift," Joe said. "For a girl. Something special."

"Ah, that's our specialty," the alien replied. "I think I may have just what you need."

After choosing the alien's suggested gift, Joe went out and followed the signs. Soon he found himself near a building in the form of a spaceship with the shining sign "Friends of the Star Baron."

When he went inside, he stopped in amazement. Massive holographic beings he did not recognize, floated across the starry space that made up the inner hall of the bar. The tables were continuously moving around, so the waiters had to fly up to them.

As Elira said, the racers were already there. Joe requested a table near the entrance that would not move making it easier to catch the moment when she entered the bar. Before he could place an order, Helga Lutto approached him.

"Joe!" she exclaimed. "Do you mind if I sit with you? I don't have many friends here."

Joe did mind, but before he could say anything, she sat down beside him.

"Jarolad of Weya," she told the waiter. "And for you…?" she asked, turning to Joe.

"Nothing for me," the young man said. "Until the race is over, I don't trust the drinks."

"Come on, you know me. I mean only to help." Helga turned to the waiter. "The same for him."

Joe looked for Elira, but she wasn't anywhere to be seen. "How did you like the first race?" Helga asked.

"Not what I imagined," Joe replied. "By the way, thanks for the help."
"Not at all," Helga replied shyly.

She moved closer to him, forcing him back to the corner of the seat.

"I really want you to win, Joe," she said. "I wish your victory even more than my own."

The waiter brought drinks. Helga stuck a twisted straw into her glass and took a sip.

"Drinks from Weya are made in a special laboratory," she said. "I've been there and seen everything. They are good for your health."

Joe took a cautious sip. A warm wave immediately passed through his body.

"There's nothing like that on Melgera," he said. "Otherwise, I'd drink it every day."

Helga moved even closer to him.

"Tell me something about yourself, Joe," she asked. "Who are the Gurts?"

Joe thought for a moment.

Before the Mega Race he could proudly describe their ideals for hours to anyone who asked, but now it seemed to him that there was nothing to tell.

"How can I put it? They live in their own little world, world of anarchy - something they call freedom - but only because they don't know any other way, you know?"

Helga nodded with understanding. Just above her shoulder, his eyes landed on Elira, who was watching them both. Having met his gaze, she turned away and disappeared into the crowd of people who were vigorously discussing the races.

"I've got to go," Joe said, jumping up and gently pushing Helga aside.

She nearly fell off her chair as he sprang from the table and raced through the crowd after Elira. When he reached her, he stood in her way.

"I've been waiting here for you for ages!"

"And it seems you weren't bored," Elira answered, crossing her arms over her chest and looking towards the table.

"Are you talking about Helga? Wait a minute," he laughed. "Do you really mean to say that you are jealous?!"

"What? Me? Why would I be?"

"Greetings to all finalists of the first qualifying round of the Star Mega Race!" A loud voice rang out from what seemed to be nowhere and everywhere at once. "Yesterday you did your best! And now it's time to take a break!"

The hall was drowned in a deafening thunder of music, and small bubbles flew from the ceiling.

"Let's get out of here," Joe said, trying to shout over the music. "I want to talk in private."

"You don't have to go far," Elira screamed.

She caught one of the bubbles and blew into it. It began to grow in size and soon devoured them both.

Joe noticed that many others there did the same. After a few moments, the bar seemed to remain behind a transparent wall, and they appeared inside the bubble.

Within it was an unfamiliar landscape from another planet. The dark sky was strewn with stars, and four moons shone, hanging over the rocks like pale disks. Nearby was a lake of silvery water and the surrounding

ground was bare apart from being peppered with craters from meteorites.

"Where are we?" Joe asked.

"These are travel bubbles with views of other planets. We can burst it and end up back in the bar. Do you want to choose another one?"

"No," said Joe. "I like it here."

They sat down on a black boulder near the water. "Tell me about your planet," Joe asked.

"It is located in the heart of X2," said Elira. "In the eastern district of Orion called P20L5. I was born there, or to be more precise, I was created from a tube."

"And your mother?" Joe asked.

"She was from the planet 73TE12, but she died. Refused to be a cyborg. As you know, X2 is a cyborg world. One day I will become one, too."

"Hmm." Joe shook his curls and lay down on a boulder, looking at the stars. "I wish I could go there. I wish I could go everywhere."

"Not me." Elira said. "I've seen so much that I'm already bored." "Is that why you always look so sad?"

The girl thought for a second.

"No, not because of that, but because I have no talents."

"Well, you probably just haven't found out what they are yet."

"My father is very rich," said Elira. "Since childhood, absolutely

everything has been available to me. I meet so many talented aliens. But I can't do anything myself. When I watch you get behind the wheel and rush to the finish line, I..."

"Are you really jealous?"

"Yes! I would also like to be able to do something. But I'm not good at anything."

"You don't need to. You inspire us with your very presence!"

"But still. That girl you were talking to, Helga, is my age, and she was in the top thirty yesterday. And me, I can't do anything. My father doesn't even allow me to study. He just keeps me here as a decoration."

"Perhaps I could change that, at least for a while." said Joe.

He carefully retrieved the gift he had chosen for her. The girl opened it and took out two small stickers. Leaning in, she kissed his cheek and stuck one on his arm, the other on hers.

The next moment they were on board the spacecraft in the control cabin. Elira laughed like a child and sat down in the captain's chair. Joe sat next to her.

"You dreamed of driving spaceships, right?" he said, switching on the control buttons.

Elira turned the steering wheel, and her eyes lit up.

They flew through star filled space. Slowly at first, circling asteroids, and then as fast as they could, reaching beyond the stars.

They seemed to have circled half the galaxy when Judd's voice rang out loudly in the middle of the spaceship.

"Elira!"

The girl jumped up from her seat, tore the sticker off her arm, and disappeared. Joe followed her.

The bubble they were in burst, and they found themselves back in the noisy bar. Judd stood in front of them.

"I expected you to communicate with all the racers, not hide somewhere with one," he said, looking at Joe, who only now noticed that the cyborg, instead of pupils, had black lights that changed color every now and then. "You must be in the photos with everyone."

"I'm sorry, sir," said the racer. "It's all my fault."

"Joe Dee Myers, 49th place," Judd said, continuing to drill him with his eyes.

"49th so far," Joe corrected him.

The cyborg turned and walked away with his robotic gait. "Thank you," Elira whispered to Joe and followed her father.

Joe looked around. Without Elira, there was absolutely nothing for him to do here. He was about to leave when, suddenly, an alien in a suit appeared in front of him.

"Joe Dee Myers," he drawled sweetly. "Do I know you?" Joe asked.

"I don't think so, but Star Baron has already placed his bets, even on things that don't involve racing. He asked me to give this to you."

He handed Joe a small gold token.

"What is this?" Joe asked, looking at the token, which bore an ornate coat of arms.

"This is a small gift. Only special friends of the Star Baron receive one. Very rare."

The alien then stepped back and vanished into thin air.

Joe didn't know what the alien was talking about, and he felt terribly tired. It was a beautiful day, but he needed to rest. He tossed the token into the air, caught it and slipped it into his pocket.

He left the bar and teleported to the hotel, where he collapsed on the bed and immediately fell asleep.

Chapter 15

Enemies of the Universe

◉

When the phone rang and the news screen appeared above his bed, Joe opened his eyes and without hesitation got up straight away; there was no need for Ulit this morning. Joe knew that it was the day of the second qualifying race, and he was more than ready to confront his opponents.

He took a shower and then went out onto the sunny terrace. The view from there gave him a sense of tranquility. A light breeze came from the ocean. A faint ringing of bells could be heard from the town on the mountainside.

"Look at this," exclaimed Ulit when he came out. "Who's the early bird here?"

"I'm ready." Joe was stretching and jumping. "Today I will tear them all apart. Mardo Keaton! Wut Hunger! They haven't seen me in all my glory yet!"

Ulit agreed, pouring him a tangy drink. But Joe lay down on the floor and started doing push-ups.

"I need to warm up before the race. Today I must come first!"

He did a hundred push-ups, a few hundred jumps, stretched on the ledge, then sat down at the table and gulped down his drink.

Ulit turned on the news.

"Today, all the eyes of the universe are turned to Agarna, where soon fifty of the best racers will enter the second qualifying round of the Interstellar Mega Race! Among them is Mardo Keaton! Wut Hunger! Marva Tanto! And many more who will compete to be the top twenty-five who will enter the final round!"

"Joe, eat something," demanded Ulit. "You'll need some strength."

Without taking his eyes off the screen, Joe stuffed several cream buns into his mouth, a porridge made of something he never tasted before, and drank a glass of juice.

"Twenty minutes before the start," he got up. "I think it's time to go." Ulit put on his jacket. A shining port appeared in front of him. "Request to the Golden Tribune," they heard.

"Go, show them, brother," said Ulit. "Remember, we both know that you are the best!"

He entered the port and disappeared.

Joe closed his eyes and, ready to be transported, said, "Pavilion." But nothing happened. Joe opened his eyes. "Pavilion!" he said again, but the port did not appear. "Hotel reception," "Market," "Bar Caterpillar." Joe

tried again and again, yet nothing happened.

"Seventh Star!" he screamed and ran out of the room.

He found himself in a long corridor and rushed forward along it, looking at every door which had large numbers that seemed to never end.

"Noooooi!"

"Yes, Joe?"

"Something strange is happening again! I can't teleport to the track!"

"Where are you?"

"In the hotel!"

"What floor?"

"315th!"

"Try to use an emergency elevator at the end of the corridor," Noi suggested.

Joe ran there as fast as he could and saw a tiny silver door. He banged on the button a hundred times, and a minute later the door opened.

An old alien lady in uniform was standing there with a trolley full of cleaning products. She gave Joe a disapproving look when he entered and pressed the lobby button ten times.

"I'm sorry, ma'am," Joe said. "Two things have plagued me since childhood - the fear of moving through the portals and claustrophobia."

The elevator was moving down, and Joe felt like an eternity had passed. It stopped at the 117th floor. The alien walked out slowly, pushing the trolley forward, and then gave Joe another frown.

"Come on," Joe yelled, frantically pushing the button as the door began to close.

As soon as he got to the lobby, he ran out of the building.

"Don't worry, Joe," said Noi. "You have twelve minutes before the race starts. You only need to cross the square, go up to the second level, and run five blocks."

"Five?"

"Racer Myers!" There was a frightening scream from Coach in his ears. "Why aren't you on the starting line? Are you hanging out in the Caterpillar Bar again?"

"Everything is under control, coach, I promise!" Joe shouted and heard the usual sound of the coach exhaling spice smoke.

He ran with all his power. Crossed the square. Three minutes. Climbed the wide stairs to the second floor. Two minutes. And then he ran through the streets of the town.

Large screens broadcasting the start of the races floated in the air all around him.

"All the racers of the second qualifying round are ready and waiting for the signal to start. But where is Joe Dee Myers?" asked the announcer from the screen.

"Indeed, he seems to be late again!"

The racers warmed up their cars hanging in the air. The wild roar of their turning wheels and turbines were heard everywhere.

"Five, four, three, two, one!"

The racing town was drowned in the noise of the crowds of fans.

"And so, at this very moment 50, no wait, 49 racing cars start! They are rushing towards the goal, ready to fight for a place in the final! But where is Joe?"

Running Joe appeared on all screens.

"There he is! Look how he runs to the race! It seems that being late has become a habit for him!" the announcers said.

"Maybe he just wants to make an impression?" another announcer asked.

"One way or another, he succeeded. According to my data, most of the spectators at the moment are not looking at the race participants, but at Joe Dee Myers, who is running around the racing town!"

They didn't have to discuss it any longer as an exhausted Joe arrived on the track.

"Lizard!" he shouted, and the car appeared in front of him.

Joe jumped in and hit all the buttons and levers at once.

"He's arrived!" The whole universe seemed to be celebrating that moment as well as the announcers. "Three minutes late, which I would say is a great result, because last time it was 11 minutes."

"Let's wish him luck!"

"Coach Pritmut," Joe gasped. "Coach Pritmut, I've started!"

"Turn the car around, you slob. You're heading towards the sun."

Joe heard a request from the racer channel, and when he switched, there was a loud laugh that seemed to never end.

"You are undoubtedly a legend, Joe," said the mocking voice of Harvey.

"He's just trying to show off." Binnie was choking with laughter.

But Joe had already caught up with the last racers. Two attacked him from the right, but he easily dodged both. He actually forced one to hit the ground. Another car flew down from above, and it knocked him off the track for a few seconds.

"656 to 215, 785 to 144, 782 to 448, and again two on the right. Concentrate," shouted Pritmut.

Joe turned on the spiral movement mode and maneuvered through the stream of cars like fish in water. More than half of them were left behind.

"747 to 122, 138 to 654. Very good, Myers. You're learning."

Joe turned on the turbines. He was pushed back into his seat with the car's sudden acceleration. He was worried that the car's shell might be melting as the air around it crackled as if it was now electrified.

"Noi, do you think the car can take it?" he asked.

"No doubt, Joe!" Noi said proudly, "Noi put over a thousand protectors, fuses and three-thousand, two-hundred pressure plates in it."

Hearing this, Joe added even more power to the levers. And after a few minutes, he broke into the top ten, and soon after he was where he wanted to be, among the top three.

"To your right is Mardo Keaton! On the left is Marva Tanto." said Pritmut. "Speed up, you must overtake Wut Hunger!"

Mardo and Marva squeezed him from the sides, but he pulled up and they collided with each other. Ahead of them loomed his target, the light blue car of Wut Hunger.

"Well done, Joe," said Wut. "I always knew you were a worthy opponent. But what do you say to this?"

A black cloud emerged from the back of Wut's car. The next moment, slime covered the Lizard's windscreen. Joe turned on the wipers, but they made it worse.

"Isn't that forbidden?" He was outraged.

"Do as I say, Joe, and don't slow down," Pritmut said. "755 to 616, 393 to 594, 155 to 270, maneuver 587!"

He continued to rattle off the settings to Joe. Travelling at speed without seeing anything or not knowing where he was heading was agony. This lasted for some minutes.

In the Golden Tribune, all eyes were on Joe.

"He's first!" Ulit exclaimed, not believing what he was seeing.

"This is where the skill of the racer merges with the skill of the coach!" Nuan said admiringly.

"Don't rush to conclusions." Barver grinned. "This is just the beginning!"

Zelga sipped her drink and studied Ulit's face with a smile. She suddenly stood up and took off Ulit's glasses, which completely took him by surprise.

"You have very beautiful features for someone who was not created in a test tube."

Ulit became uncomfortable. He gently reclaimed his glasses, put them on, and turned back to the screen.

Joe slowed down and braked sharply at the coach's direction. "Land! And tell Noi he has 54 seconds to wash the car."

The Lizard disappeared. Joe was left alone on the ground in the middle of the desert. He peered at the horizon, the cars he overtook were far behind, but some of them were already approaching. Wut Hunger flew right over his head.

Suddenly, the ground beneath Joe's feet began to crack. A little at first, then more. He took a step back.

"Run," the coach yelled.

And Joe, acting on impulse, rushed forward, jumping over the cracks that appeared in his path. One of them it turned out was too wide. He slipped, grabbing the edge of the ground, and turned to see the crack growing, exposing an abyss below.

Above him, racing cars continued to fly past. Some of them crashed into the rocks that were growing out of the ground in front of them.

"Climb up!" barked the coach.

Joe scrambled up, but as soon as he rose to the surface, he saw one of the racing cars heading straight at him. The blast that it created hit him in the chest and he started to fall.

"Lizard!" Joe shouted and he immediately hit its roof as it hovered in the air. He rolled to one side trying to get nearer to the door.

"How long will you hang there, loser? You've slipped to 35th place!" yelled Pritmut.

Joe grabbed the edge of the door, then reached up and crawled inside.

The glass was clean but still covered with soapy water that Noi apparently didn't have time to wipe off.

"All levers to full, 812 to 357, 718 to 324 and turn 360!"

Joe flew up above the cracked, rock-strewn ground. He again overtook cars one by one and soon got back closer to Wut.

Suddenly the Lizard got glued to the ground. It appeared to be moving up and down.

Joe looked around. He was not alone. About a dozen racers were also stuck here, in a place that reminded him of an amusement park. Above, a massive robot with long legs and a wide smile, was busy hitting cars with a giant hammer. If they did not have time to get out of the way the blow would certainly fall right on them as he aimed well.

For a moment, Joe froze not knowing how to deal with this situation. He had already witnessed two racers getting wacked, but when the robot turned towards him, he just screamed.

"Get out now!" shouted Pritmut.

"Noi, take the Lizard!" Joe shouted as he jumped out of the car.

The robot hit an empty spot and laughed, but he didn't give up. He followed Joe, who was now running, trying to hit him with a hammer until the young man found a large iron wall to hide behind.

He wanted to call the Lizard but noticed something that stopped him. "Helga?" he exclaimed, seeing the girl hiding in the same place. He approached.

"I'm scared," she said, sitting down and covering her head with her hands.

Joe didn't know what to do. He touched her shoulder with his hand, and then lightly hugged her.

"It's fine," he said. "Let's go, otherwise we'll both come last." She nodded and got up, still trembling and looking around. "Ray!" she shouted.

Her car immediately appeared.

"What just happened?" Joe exclaimed as he climbed back inside the Lizard.

"Are you talking about a girl or a robot?" Pritmut asked sarcastically, and then yelled as loud as he could, "Are you out of your mind to help other racers?! Wut Hunger is already far ahead of you!"

With that one thought, all of Joe's strength returned to him, and he flew forward almost at the speed of light. He was again overtaking cars and maneuvering between the obstacles that challenged all his skills and

reactions to the limit.

"Do you like this girl?" asked Pritmut suddenly. "No, I like the other one," Joe replied.

"Elira Bright?"

"How do you know?"

"Coach Pritmut knows everything about everything," the slug replied.

"We're going to get married when I win. We'll buy a house somewhere in the Western part of Orion. Children and all that."

"Ahh," drawled the coach. "What sweet dreams. But right now you're back in 25th place."

"Woo-hoo," Joe exclaimed happily. "That's almost the first."

At that moment, the trunk of a car in front of him opened and a shower of metal discs shot out right onto the Lizard. However, Joe's reaction was lightning fast. He moved up and the discs damaged the car

behind him instead.

"That's Binnie Juice," said Pritmut. "His brother is waiting for you 200 meters on the left."

Joe turned right.

"Binnie's on the right again."

"Are they playing games with me?" Joe exclaimed indignantly.

"It seems so," Coach answered. "Let's try to outwit them. 757 to 434,175 to 285. Maneuver 547, 938, 273."

And Joe, like lightning, began to move between the obstacles and cars, attacking the Juice brothers, who were trying to drive him into a trap. But soon, not being able to compete with Joe, they were both left behind.

"I did good, Coach, didn't I?" Joe whistled with pride. "Not as good as I did, Myers."

"Come on, Coach. You must give me at least some credit!"

The landscape then changed again and the Lizard was being doused with water that spread to the horizon.

"The water monsters of planet Shira," Pritmut said. "One wrong move, Myers, and you'll be flattened."

Joe screamed when the bulky water figures appeared in front of him. They were trying to grab the car but falling back into the water, they would dissolve and disappear. There were so many of them, and they appeared so suddenly that his view was rendered useless, but the coach was his eyes, and that saved him.

"Do you want me to give you credit here as well?" asked Pritmut when the water monsters were left behind.

"No but I have a question to ask."

"Go ahead, smarty."

"Why wouldn't you participate?" Pritmut exhaled the smoke.

"You got me there, Myers. Let's just say as sad as it sounds, some are built for one thing, others for another. For me, the reason I became a coach was an attempt to fix a broken dream."

Joe felt bad for asking.

"Stop digging into the past. There is a mirror tunnel ahead of you."

"Seventh star! What is that?"

But before Joe could hear the answer, he saw hundreds of reflections of his car that were moving in different directions, and he had no idea where the racetrack was.

"Just do what I say," the coach commanded.

His voice was clear and insistent as he dictated the settings, and the racer did his best to keep up. It lasted so long that at some point, it began to feel like he was no longer in the car, but somewhere in another reality, where all that mattered was following commands and switching settings.

"Open your eyes, Joe," said the coach, slightly out of breath. "The tunnel is behind us now."

Joe looked at the scenery that changed and whistled with delight.

"All I can say, coach, is that you fixed your dream well," said Joe in admiration.

Everyone in the Golden Tribune rejoiced.

"How easily they passed the mirror tunnel!" Marken applauded loudly. The others joined him.

"For Pritmut who is back in the game." Nuan proposed the toast,

clinking glasses with everyone, "Could Joe really be his seventh champion?"

"Be careful. Do not jinx it," Zelga laughed. "The fate of all the planets of the periphery is at stake."

"Even if I don't agree with it politically, I have to admit in my heart even I'm for Joe," said Barver.

But suddenly a loud scream was heard. Everyone turned around. An alien appeared in the center of the Golden Tribune. He'd just teleported in and seemed out of breath.

"The Lagrians are spreading evil!" he squealed as loudly as he could. "They are the enemies of the Universe!"

"Who let this madman in?" Barver frowned.

The intruder continued.

"They teleport darkness throughout the universe! Agreements with Lagra will lead to Orion's death! We must stop them before it's too late!"

At this point, several security personnel arrived to deal with the situation, they ran up to him, twisted his arms, and teleported him away.

"It's a shame," said Marken. "I would have liked to have heard him out."

"Who cares what a lunatic thinks?" Barver chuckled.

"But Dormart was the first to sign a contract with Lagra," Nuan pointed out accusingly.

"An agreement with the Lagrians, not with Lagra," Zelga corrected. "Maldoran would not have agreed if the others had not put pressure on it."

"Do you really want to discuss political affairs?" Barver asked angrily.

"Calm down," Marken said. "That's not what we're here for. Let's focus on the race."

"Fine," Nuan agreed. "But don't forget that neither of us has been to Lagra, and it is already taking control of certain parts of Orion."

Ulit was confused, understanding almost nothing. He fought for his planet Melgera for such a long time that knew almost nothing about politics of Orion, and these talks about danger coming from "god's district," as it was called, made him worried.

"Sand City on Planet Reiki," said the coach.

The landscape had already changed as Joe drove into a huge city.

The grotesque ruins of buildings stretched so high up that their roofs could not be seen.

"At least it looks beautiful," said tired Joe, yawning.

He flew through the gaps in the buildings that used to be windows. The walls began to collapse, raising massive clouds of sandy dust up into the air, but Joe managed to escape the destruction.

"Ahead of you is Marva Tanto," the coach said. "It seems she is up to something."

The girl maneuvered between the buildings and destroyed them in front of Joe. She did it in such a manner that the young man was barely able to even notice her car. At some point, she drove him into a dead end, then blocked the path with her car and pressed him against the wall. Joe looked up, the wall was collapsing above him, ready to fall and crush him right there.

"You're an upstart, a nobody," she said with her caustic voice. "And you'll stay here forever!"

"As far as I remember, you said that I wouldn't make it even to the second round," the racer answered and switched the channel. "Noi, take the car."

The Lizard disappeared and Joe began falling down into the sandy unknown.

"Lizard!" he shouted.

The car reappeared. He rolled over the roof and climbed inside, a maneuver he was now familiar with, and managed to dodge the falling wall. Joe was not going to leave that trick unanswered. He caught up with Marva Tanto and cut the side of her car with a razor that appeared from Lizard's hood as he overtook her. The girl lost control and disappeared in a cloud of sandy dust.

"Do you think we should look for her, Coach?"

"She switched to a parallel track," answered Pritmut. "A stupid decision in my opinion, but to our advantage."

Joe pressed on, avoiding the last remaining collapsing buildings. The scenery then began to change.

There were massive piles of rubbish all around, drifting in one direction. The Lizard flew past them, slicing through the air. The danger was not immediately apparent but then the car began to drift to the right.

"Valley of the winds from planet 7L20," said Pritmut, "Here I am no use. Act on your intuition and try not to be blown away."

The Lizard was flailing from side to side and Joe, who was being thrown around the cabin, could barely manage to control it. At some point, he almost flew into a mountain of debris, but, fortunately for him,

another stream of air swept him up just in time.

Just when it seemed like that was too much to handle, something strange fell on the Lizard's windshield, followed by another. The racer took a closer look - they were small humanoid robots.

"The scavengers," said Pritmut. "They are designed to take large structures apart."

"Like my car?" Joe yelled as one of them ripped off a piece of Lizard's metal covering.

He turned the car on its side, trying to shake off the robots. But one by one they continued to stick to it, tearing it to pieces. Joe opened the window and hit one of them, then another, but more and more appeared.

"Try a corkscrew maneuver," Pritmut said.

The Lizard spun and the centrifugal force managed to loosen the robots grip.

Joe was unable to stop screaming. The Lizard crossed an invisible barrier and flew into a starry space above the surface of an unknown planet. The car slowly circled among the stars. Inside, Joe's head was spinning.

"Gravity has disappeared," Pritmut stated thoughtfully, deciding what to do.

Joe saw three more racers ahead. They slowly rotated in space, turning over on their axis. The next thing the young man noticed was that the air in the car was depleting.

"Joe," Noi said carefully. "You asked for the feature 25XC. It creates a gravitational field. To activate it, set 912 to 70."

"Seventh Star!" Joe breathed out a sigh of relief. "Why didn't you tell me sooner, Noi?"

The car surged forward.

"What are you doing, Myers?" shouted Pritmut.

"It's all right, Coach," Joe said breathlessly. "We'll get out of here in no time!"

"I don't think I told you to do that!"

But it was already too late. Joe flew straight into an invisible wall. Reality was torn apart, and the Lizard found itself in a raging river.

The racer lost control. Water filled the cabin of the car. In a few seconds, he was carried away towards a precipice that stretched along the entire horizon, as far as his eyes could see.

The Lizard creaked plaintively and flew down the endless waterfall. Joe choked, but Noi, apparently realizing that he would not get his command, took the car. And now Joe was falling in a powerful stream of water. He landed in a lake, sank to the bottom, and lost consciousness.

It seemed that he had spent an eternity there in dense darkness, when the Star Stadium in Gurt city floated before his mind's eye.

The crowds shouted, "Joe! Joe! Joe! Dee! Dee! Dee! Myyyyyyers!" He couldn't let them down. But where was he? Suddenly he remembered, opened his eyes, and inhaled water. That didn't stop him. He kicked off the bottom with his feet and swam up using all his might.

"Spectacular, but cruel." Zelga was sipping her cocktail and yawning.

"This year there are already twice as many victims as usual," Nuan agreed.

"And, in my opinion, the Lagrians added some sparkle." Barver ate nuts.

As for Ulit, he froze in place, looking at the screen. His heart was beating fast, and his hands were shaking as he waited for Joe to come to the surface, but this did not happen. He couldn't bear the fear and shock he experienced and screamed as loud as he could.

"Don't you understand that they are dying?! They just die there, and that's it! This is no longer a sport! This is a fight for survival!"

"Shhhh. Quiet." Marken touched him on the shoulder. "50 billion on Joe surviving this obstacle."

The bet got accepted and as Marken predicted, Joe emerged to the water surface to the loud applause of the hall.

"Told you," Marken licked a slice of an orange. "500 billion for Joe to be in the top three. I seem to have more faith in your brother than you do."

A small translucent screen immediately flashed on and off in front of him.

"Why don't you make bets too?" asked Barver, turning to Ulit. "So much fun!"

Ulit couldn't believe it. They seem to not care. He left them and walked around the hall, but everywhere he went, he saw only aliens making bets.

Joe coughed nonstop as he reached the shore. He could not figure out what the coach was shouting. He just lay down on the ground and looked at the sky that was changing colors. There was a bird soaring above him, which made him realize that he was still alive.

"Get up, Racer Myers, now," Pritmut insisted.
"To hell with it, I can't," Joe answered, still coughing.

"If you lie here and whine like Varya's seals, you will remain a loser for the rest of your days."

But Joe didn't move.

"What about the Bright girl? Did you notice the way Wut Hunger looked at her at the conference? I noticed. He couldn't take his eyes off her! But he is now in the lead, and just imagine how she will look at him when he comes first?"

That did the trick as Joe lifted his head off the ground and slowly stood up. He was still staggering and felt dizzy.

"Lizard," he shouted.

The car appeared in front of him.

"Noi pumped out the water as much as he could, but residual moisture can still have a negative effect," Noi said. "And Joe, Noi is so sorry."

But Joe was already in the car, pulling his racing goggles over his eyes.

"500 to 177, 400 to 547."

The racer was moving forward through the changing landscape.

"Coach, it was Wut Hunger who told me about the 25XC function. Could he know what waits for us on the track?"

"The only thing that matters, Myers, is that you were smart enough to listen to him but not smart enough to ask me. Here, only I give orders!"

"Got it," Joe answered. "Do you know who Star Baron is?" "What does this have to do with it?"

"He said I was his friend."

"Don't make me laugh, Myers, Star Baron has no friends."

Barriers and obstacles appeared in front of Joe so suddenly that he barely had time to dodge them. Among these obstacles, massive clouds of darkness appeared; at first little by little, then more and more often.

"Don't look at it and don't think about it," Pritmut ordered, as if he could feel Joe's gaze lingering on the endless black masses. "You must overcome Mardo Keaton, who is ahead of you!"

A few minutes passed for what felt like an eternity to Joe, and Mardo Keaton's yellow-and-black car started to loom ahead.

"He won't give in to you that easily," Pritmut warned.

It was true. When Joe almost caught up with him, Mardo hit the Lizard so hard that it flew off to the side and fell behind.

"Next time, be more careful."

Joe increased speed and leveled with Keaton again.

"His mechanic is exceptional," said the racer, unable to overtake him.

They scraped each other with such force that coating of both cars caught fire from friction and fell away.

Joe's head was buzzing, and the blood was rushing to his temples, but he knew he couldn't give up.

As a cloud of darkness appeared in front of them, both racers parted to opposite sides, but they soon came back together again, pushing each other in turn with increasing force. Another barrier appeared and Mardo

deviated to the left, which gave Joe an advantage, and he pulled ahead.

However, further along Keaton overtook him again and hit him so hard that both cars spun together and fell to the ground, tumbling sideways. Something forcefully pushed Joe in the side, and he began to lose consciousness from the shock of pain.

"Racer Myers!" Coach yelled, and Joe opened his eyes.

He was lying upside down in an overturned car, with Keaton's yellow-and-black car burning on the side.

"Get up now," commanded Pritmut.

Joe looked down and saw a piece of iron sticking out of his side and blood streaming down the seat of the car. He slowly lifted his hands to the air.

"574 to 360, 155 to 340." Pritmut loudly inhaled the smoke, "you must finish before he comes to his senses!"

The Lizard was making cracking sounds. With his last strength, Joe followed the coach's orders. Everything became blurry. He was almost losing consciousness. A few minutes passed and he drove into a white wall of light.

"You have crossed the first barrier," said Pritmut.

The impenetrable black wall rose before Joe's eyes again, and he was unable to drag his gaze away from it.

"Break, Myers!"

Joe was racing forward at full speed when Pritmut screamed again in such a way that it hurt the racer's eardrums.

"I said, stop, now!"

Joe hit the brakes. The car did three somersaults in the air and landed just over a thin, hardly visible line.

"You've crossed the second barrier." Pritmut exhaled the smoke in relief.

The young man looked at his stomach. An iron rod was protruding from his side. He pulled it out carefully and pressed his hand to the wound.

Slowly he got out of the car, leaving behind a pool of blood. Every muscle in his body trembled. He looked at the Lizard or rather, what was left of it, and then on the wall of darkness in front of him. How beautiful and charming it was.

This thought faded and so did his consciousness.

Chapter 16

Amendment 7712

The light was so bright that it pierced through and dissolved everything that was in its way. Luminous creatures gradually came into view; they were even brighter.

"Where am I?" Joe asked.

"In Lagra, my friend," one of the creatures answered. "The world of the gods."

The light flooded in again and drowned out everything.

"The wound was deep indeed. Poor fellow," someone said above him. "Too many of them died this year."

"I wonder how many will survive the main race."

Joe opened his eyes. It wasn't Lagra at all. Three cyborgs, two men and one woman, stood over him and moved strange devices over his stomach.

"Are you awake?" one of them carefully asked. "Seventh star. Where am I?" Joe was wincing in pain.

"In the hospital of the racers' town," answered the cyborg. "I'm Doctor F425, and these are Doctors D7N40 and LK917. We brought you back to life."

Joe looked at the smooth skin on his side without a hint of injury. "There is nothing?"

"You people are easy to patch up, but also easy to damage." said doctor F425. "I strongly recommend switching to the cyborg model of existence."

"I'll pass on that," Joe said, trying to get up.

"I don't think moving is a good idea. After the painful shock you experienced and such a complex healing operation, it is recommended to stay in bed for at least 17 days."

"I don't have 17 days," Joe answered. "What day is it today?! How did I finish?!"

The doctors looked at each other.

"Coach Pritmut!" Joe shouted, "Coach Pritmut!"

"We finished third," he heard familiar voice say in his ears. "But you won't go to the final race."

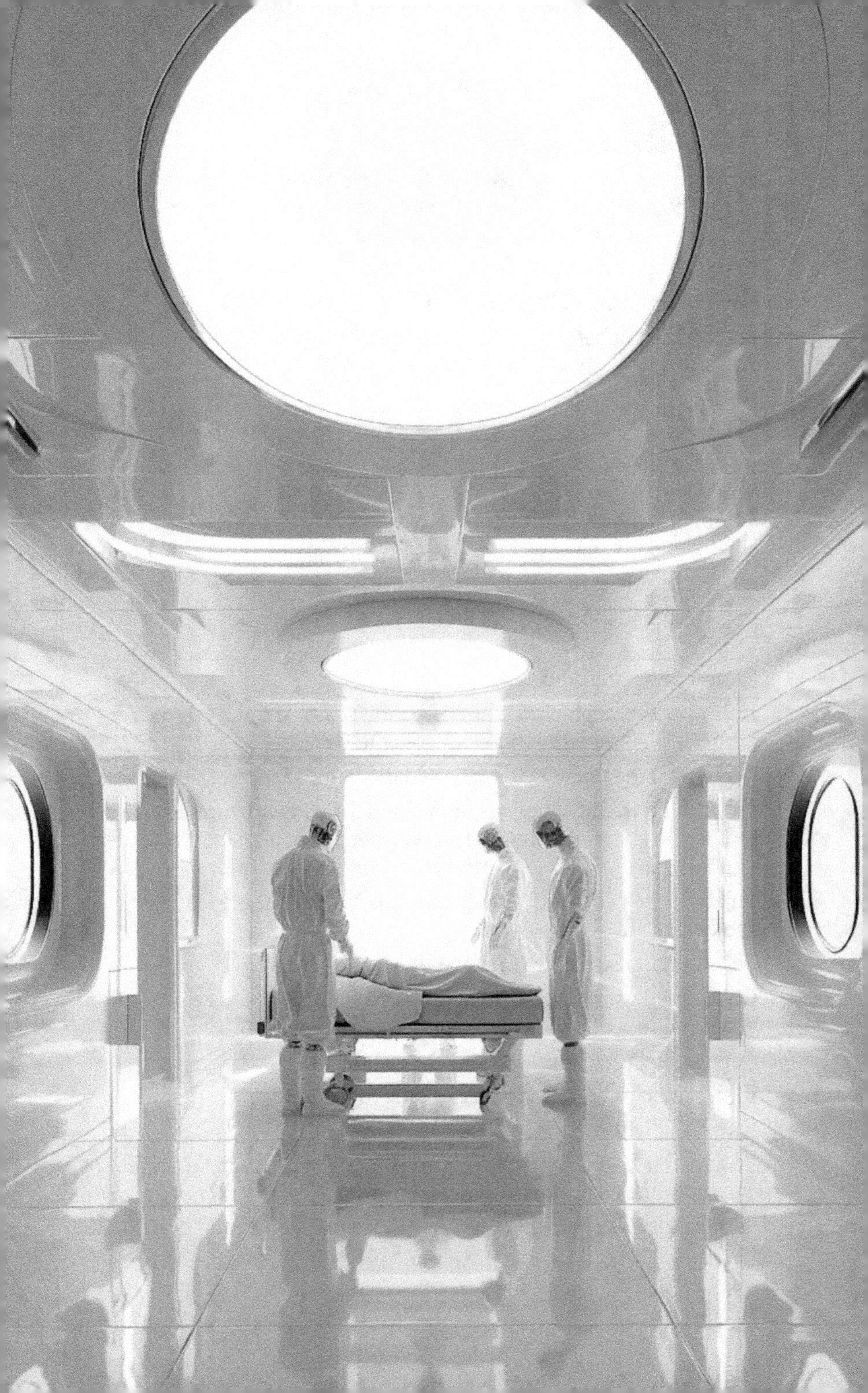

"But..." Joe began to choke with indignation.

"You survived a very serious operation, boy. You won't be able to handle the third round. Thank the universe that you survived. Now pack your things and go back to Melgera."

The coach disconnected.

"No!" Joe exclaimed. "No! No! No!"

He rolled out of bed and started crawling across the floor towards the exit.

"Hotel!" he shouted.

"You can't teleport right now," D7N40 said, lifting him up with a small device and placing him back on the bed. "Not until you're fully recovered."

Ulit ran into the ward, and the doctors left.

"I'm sorry, Joe!" Ulit said, almost crying. "It's all my fault! I made you go to these stupid races!"

"Ulit, I'm fine!" shouted Joe. "Better tell me why I'm not allowed to the final?!"

Ulit nervously adjusted his glasses.

"There was so much blood that they didn't even show it on the screens. We all thought you were going to die!"

"But I'm not the only one who would die in these races, right?"

"That is why we must go back home and forget everything like a bad dream!" He lowered his voice to a whisper. "The Lagrians made the races too dangerous! Many people don't like this anymore."

"I'm not those people! I'd rather die than not participate!" But Ulit shook his head.

"Only 24 participants reached the finish line."

"This is one less than expected." Joe was delighted. "Less competition in the final round."

"You won't participate," Ulit said firmly. "I will!"

"After that operation, you won't be able to! This is certain death!"

"I can and I will participate."

Ulit sighed. He stood up, made a circle around the room, and then sat down at the edge of Joe's bed again.

"I almost lost you, Joe, and Mom... No one will let you do that. I signed the papers for you. After all, you are not yet 18."

Joe was so shocked and frustrated that he couldn't speak. He needed a few moments to collect his thoughts.

"You won't do it," he finally said. "Already done."

Ulit stood up and took a few steps back.

"It's done," he repeated. "They won't change that."

"Then get out!" shouted Joe. He threw all the pillows at his brother. "Get out and never ever talk to me again!"

Ulit stood still, not knowing what to say, but when he saw tears in his brother's eyes, he turned and ran out.

Joe lay in pain. But it was not his wound. He was in the top three! He made it to the finish line! He almost won! Why did they have a right to stop him, to tell him what to do?

"Noi," he called, almost crying.

"Yes, Joe," the alien answered sadly. "How is the Lizard?"

"It's just a car. Noi can fix it."

Joe sniffled.

"Did you like the second round?"

"Everyone liked it, Joe. Check out the news."

Joe turned on the screens. Before his eyes, residents from all over Orion and its periphery discussed the races and watched the highlights. They chanted the names of the finalists. Their houses, as well as their clothes, were decorated with the faces of Wut Hunger, Marva Tanto, and Joe.

The young man smiled as he felt their abundant love and admiration. "Why did they lock me in here then? Why can't I decide for myself?" "Everybody wants Joe Dee Myers to live. And Noi himself really wants

this, too."

"The second round of the Interstellar Mega Race was more exciting than ever and weeded out more than half of the participants," the announcer said. "It is still not known how many of those who passed to the third round will participate. Finalists Wut Hunger and Marva Tanto were not seriously injured, but Joe Dee Myers, who managed to overtake Mardo Keaton and came third, is currently in the hospital. His participation is still in question, as is the life of the racer. The top ten finalists also include the Juice brothers, Helga Lutto and..." he continued to list the names.

"Wut Hunger knows what happens on the track," said Joe.

"It is possible," replied Noi. "His father is one of the main sponsors of the event."

"They disabled my teleports."

"I agree. This is vile."

"But I can still win the third round!"

"I'm afraid your brother has already decided everything for you."

In anger, Joe pushed one of the gadgets near him, it squeaked. Doctor LK917 entered the room.

"Prepare the Lizard, Noi!" shouted Joe. "Get it ready!" But the mechanic was silent.

"A girl wants to talk to you," said LK917. "She's been waiting for you for a long time."

A warm wave passed through Joe's body. He quickly tried to smooth his curls and prepare but when Helga entered the room, he almost exclaimed in frustration and relaxed with disappointment.

She was holding electronic flowers that changed colors. As she approached, she put them in a vase, collected pillows from the floor, and sat on the edge of his bed.

"How are you feeling, Joe?"

"Never felt better."

"I heard you won't participate."

"I will!" he interrupted her sharply. "I will participate!"

"Good," Helga said. "Because they're celebrating that you're out." Joe punched pillows in anger.

"I came to say thank you. There on the track, you saved me."

"You would do the same," Joe said. "can't believe you were scared of an iron robot."

"Who was trying to kill me, though."

Helga smiled and then hesitated, as if considering whether to say something or not.

"What?" Joe asked.

"They told me you want to leave Melgera," she said carefully. "It's very good on my planet. Northern Grathea is a wonderful place. And Livarda is one of the best planets in our system. My family would be happy to help you."

"I don't need help, Helga," Joe said rudely. The girl lowered her eyes.

"Thank you for your concern, but I will find my place in life myself."

"You know she's not for you," Helga said suddenly. "Besides, why is she so good?"

"I hope you're talking about my planet now," Joe said. Helga stood up and headed to the exit.

"In the final race, we will no longer be friends."

Joe shrugged.

"It seems they won't let me there anyway."

Helga wanted to say something, but changed her mind and left the room.

Once alone, Joe got up and, barely keeping his balance, approached the door. It was locked, as well as the windows.

The racer returned to bed and laid there until the evening, watching the news, where photos and videos of him would be seen every now and again. He learned about the protest movement that evolved, claiming

justice for the planets of periphery, and the role he played in it. Joe knew they needed him as well as he needed them.

He waited and waited hoping for them to come and let him participate. But time passed, nothing happened, and Joe fell asleep.

"Joe," he heard through a dream. "Wake up, Joe!"

The racer opened his eyes. It was dark. Only the dim light of a night lamp illuminated the room.

"Elira!" The racer almost jumped up, but the girl put her finger to her lips.

He couldn't help it and hugged her. He felt like he'd lost his best friend and hadn't seen her for a hundred years, and now she was right in front of him.

"Why didn't you come earlier? I was waiting for you more than for the third race."

The girl blushed slightly.

"My father doesn't want me to talk to you." Joe exhaled in disappointment.

"I'll tell you honestly: many people don't want you to go to the final," Elira said in a whisper. "They are putting pressure on the Interstellar Committee, again raising the question of the legitimacy of your participation. But they were taken completely by surprise, and did not expect that you would come third. And now it's too late to cancel anything. All the planets of the periphery, and many influential systems, want your victory. Because of you, strong political discussions have begun in Orion."

"So I must race! If only it weren't for my brother! I can't believe he let me down at the very last moment!"

Elira wanted to say something but hesitated, and Joe could see that. "Your brother doesn't decide anything," she said carefully.

Joe frowned.

"But I'm only 16. He is responsible for my guardianship, isn't he?"

"Not in the Race. There are many amendments to the Interstellar Committee agreement."

"So he deceived me?"

"He's trying to protect you, Joe. But are you really able to participate?"

"Seventh star! I am as healthy as Melgerian buffalo," Joe exclaimed and slapped his hand on his side. "You see, there's nothing!"

"Well, then all you have to tell the doctors is that you are using Amendment 7712 of the Racer's agreement with the Interstellar Committee."

"What does it say?"

"If you don't fight for your own benefit, you can invoke your right to decide your fate in the race."

"Seventh star!"

It took a few moments for Joe to realize what she did for him. "Saving people. That's what it is," he said in awe.

"What?"

"Your talent. Now we both know it." Elira smiled.
"I'm worried for you, Joe."

"Come on," the racer replied. "You'll see. I'll take first place, and we'll remember all our lives that it was only thanks to you!"

Suddenly, Elira took his hand in hers and Joe stopped laughing.

"Promise me that after the race is over, you will take me away from X2… Promise me that we will run away together! There is still a lot that you don't know about my father, about X2, and what awaits Orion in the future!"

Joe's heart was beating fast.

"I promise," he said firmly.

He gently pulled her towards him, and she lay down next to him.

"With my winnings, after water for Melgera, of course, the first thing I will do is buy a spaceship. The fastest and most powerful the universe has ever seen. And we will rush along the periphery of Orion to where Lagra is located."

"Mmm." Elira drawled dreamily.

"We'll talk to the gods. Discuss this and that. They will give us a piece of land somewhere in the most heavenly part of their world."

"We will build a house."

"Huge mansion. And we'll start a family. Ten to fifteen children." "They will all be racers."

"Yeah. They'll drive their little racing cars around the perimeter of Lagra until the gods find something better for them to do."

Elira lifted her head up and looked straight into Joe's eyes. He got closer to her face and gently kissed her lips.

For a few moments he hugged her tightly before she stood up and moved towards the exit.

"I really want you to come first, Joe," she said. "So much depends on it."

"I will. I promise!"

She smiled and left the room.

Joe had never felt so good in his entire life. It was even better than the attention of the crowds, better than winning the race. He felt as if his whole being was filled with light and warmth. This was the first time he had experienced love.

Dreaming of a wonderful future ahead of him, he fell asleep.

In the morning, doctors F425 and LK917 examined Joe and ran various devices over his body. The racer waited for them to finish with a big smile on his face.

"External and internal tissues have grown together well," F425 stated. "But you should not disturb them in the next two weeks."

"What kind of entertainment do you prefer during your stay?" asked LK917. "We have many reality simulators which will make time fly by quickly."

"Amendment 7712," Joe said curtly.

The doctors looked at each other. A translucent screen appeared before their eyes, across which lines, letters and numbers ran at great speed.

"They say a lot about you," F425 said. "I myself watched the races glued to the screens. I'd tell you now that this show isn't worth risking your life for, but that's not why you're here, right? You're free to go."

Joe quickly got out of bed and put on his suit.

"Racing Pavilion," he thought, and in the next moment, he was standing there.

Most of the racers were warming up their cars. In the distance, Joe saw Binnie and Harvey, who froze for a few moments when they saw him. But then, smiling wickedly, they waved to him. He waved back at them as if they were good old friends.

Mardo Keaton and Marva Tanto gave Joe cold looks. On the sponsor's place, Wut Hunger was talking to Elira. That was not what Joe wanted to see, but he was going to race again, and that cheered him up.

"Noi," he called.

But there was no answer. Joe walked around the perimeter.

"I know you are there," he said. "I know that you are sitting in your workshop and waiting for me to call you. I also know that you have already repaired the Lizard. I know that because you and I are of the same kind. We are racers! Racing is everything to us, isn't it? Only I drive the car, and you repair it. But the only thing that matters to us is forward movement, towards the finish line. Isn't it?"

He paused.

"Come on, Noi!" thought Joe. "Respond!" He waited a few moments more.

"Noi almost fixed it," the alien said quietly. "Almost." Joe jumped for joy.

"Well done, Noi! There's still some time before the start. Will you make it?"

"Noi will. It'll be even better than new, Joe. But what about you?"

"I'm already better than new," Joe replied. "Are you kidding? These cyborg guys from X2 fixed me in just 24 hours. But tell me that you are with me?!"

"Noi is always with Joe Dee Myers. He saw his talent a long time ago at the Gurt stadium. But Pritmut..."

"Leave him to me!" Joe exclaimed.

He looked so happy that he attracted attention. Binnie and Harvey approached.

"Big brother let little Joe go racing?" said Binnie mockingly.

"That's exactly what happened, if you want to know," replied Joe. "Very well," said Harvey. "But it's a pity that the Coach Pritmut has

already left the racing town."

Joe didn't expect that and couldn't hide his disappointment. Binnie and Harvey looked at each other and then laughed.

"You didn't know. Did you?"

Joe managed the most carefree smile he could, but they laughed even harder and left.

Joe was thinking hard. It was too late to run after Pritmut if he left. Did the coach really abandon him?

"Coach Pritmut," he called. "I just wanted to say that I used amendment 7712. And Noi is back on the team."

But there was no answer.

"I can't go alone. Or rather, I can, but I can't win!" But the channel seemed empty.

"Coach Pritmut, without you, I'll be the last to arrive!" Joe yelled as loud as he could.

Racers turned around. Some looked at him with sympathy. Joe kicked a nearby banner.

"Whatever! I'll go alone!"

He turned on the screen, which immediately appeared in front of him in the air, and began to watch the news.

"Joe! Joe! Joe! Dee! Dee! Dee! Myyyyyyyers!!!" chanted the crowds all over the universe.

"According to the latest data, Joe Dee Myers has recovered from the injury he received in the second round of the Interstellar Mega Race and is ready to participate in the third!" the announcer said.

On the screen, Joe saw himself walking around the perimeter of the pavilion. It was the moment he was talking to Noi.

"However, Coach Pritmut Walsh left the racing town this morning. Does it mean that Joe will race alone? Nobody doubts he is a skillful racer, but no one has ever won the Race without a coach before."

"So it's true," Joe thought and turned off the channel.

He sat in the pavilion for about an hour, watching the racers getting ready. Coaches and relatives were with them. And he was alone. But Joe was not afraid. All he wanted was just to get behind the wheel and feel the speed again.

Finally, racers began to leave the pavilion. Joe braced himself, took one last look at Elira, who smiled back at him, and followed the crowd of racers to the starting line.

Chapter 17

The Final Race

The Final Mega Race was about to start. The preliminary half an hour seemed to last forever. Joe was sitting in the car waiting to get moving while the whole world was staring at him, expecting a show of a lifetime.

It was hot, boring and a little scary, but in his mind, he was already on the road, overcoming obstacles one after another.

With nothing else to do, Joe watched the race coordinator, explaining the what, how, and why of everything to the important personalities. Perhaps in time, when he couldn't race anymore, such a profession would suit him.

He examined the Lizard. It looked awesome. All the screens and levers, and upholstery, too, shone like new. Even the bird-lizard painting on the hood was brighter than before. Noi did his best.

Joe looked out of the window. There was a smell of dust and sand, and in the distance, the desert stretched to the horizon.

"Racer Myers," came the familiar deep voice in Joe's ears, followed by spice smoke. "I can't believe you aren't late."

"Coach Pritmut!" exclaimed the young man.

"So you decided to ignore our opinion and go back to the track?"

"That's right, Coach, and I'm ready to fight for the victory like never ever before!"

"I won't say I'm happy about it," Pritmut exhaled smoke into Joe's ears again. "But your brother convinced me that leaving you would be a bigger mistake than trying to bring you to the finish line."

"So you're back!"

"Life is a racetrack, too, Joe. Our solutions are like car settings. Let's give them a hard time and finish first!"

Joe mentally thanked Ulit, then pulled on his racing goggles and looked at the road ahead of him. Huge numbers appeared.

"Five, four, three, two, one!"

All the cars accelerated at once creating a cloud of dust that filled the air leaving the stadium, no longer visible, behind them.

"The sun is behind you," said Pritmut. "Move forward at full speed!"

Joe overtook one car after another and immediately took the lead.

"This is what happens when Joe Dee Meyers is not late," the announcer said on the news. "Despite his recent injury, he is back in the game and is determined to win at all costs!"

Ulit was back at the Golden Tribune again watching the races. He was exhausted and pale.

"Shame on you." Barver turned to him with a glass of sparkling drink. "You tried to deprive us of such a spectacle!"

"He almost died!" Ulit reminded him.

"With current medicine, it is hard to die." Nuan looked excited.

"You just don't know what it's like to watch your own brother fight to the death." Zelga lightly touched Ulit's shoulder.

"I'll try to imagine," Marken said. "750 billion Kharts for Joe's victory." The screen flashed on and off.

"You see, now I will fear for his life more than for my own."

Joe was driving through huge gates that stretched high up into space. "The city of Lurs," said Pritmut. "Now the obstacles will begin."

Out of nowhere arose a city. Joe had never seen anything like this before. Buildings intertwined with each other, creating intricate patterns, and roads were twisted into serpent-like spirals. Pools of water appeared in front of him hanging in the air, and ghostly pedestrians and animals appeared sporadically in his path.

"837 to 65, 522 to 356, 437 to 280," Pritmut dictated.

And Joe, with the speed of a bullet, darted through the city, dodging every obstacle.

"Wut Hunger is only a mile behind, "Marva Tanto is in the top five," said the coach. "Mardo Keaton is right next to you."

Mardo's car cut Joe, and he braked so hard that the Lizard rolled over in the air three times before driving back onto the track.

"What are you afraid of?" the coach asked.

At that moment, Wut Hunger hit the Lizard hard in the side, but Joe turned sharply and knocked his car out of the way. Hunger flew through the window of the building and stayed behind.

"That's better!"

A few minutes passed and the landscape began to change. Lava floated and poured through the air coming from large towering rocks that grew all around.

"The Lava Valleys of the planet Chur," said Pritmut. "Here, your attention is not the only thing that matters."

"What else?" Joe asked.

Suddenly a beast like he had never seen before jumped on the hood of his car. It was covered with thick black skin that even lava could not corrode and burning red eyes that popped out of their sockets. Joe screamed as he tilted the car and tried to shake him off.

"Styphs," Pritmut explained. "These creatures have very tenacious paws. They will hang on even if we go into a tailspin."

"What do these creatures eat?" Joe asked as he escaped the lava flows.

"Guess!"

The creature opened its mouth with five rows of sharp teeth and squealed so loudly that Joe screwed up his face. The monster hit the left side window with all its might, and then again and again until a crack appeared.

Something suddenly hit Lizard's left side. Joe turned. It was Marva Tanto's car. It also had a styph on it. Joe turned, put on speed, and hit Tanto's car with his left side. His styph almost fell off but somehow managed to cling on. They both realized that it was working and swirled in the air, alternately hitting each other.

"Good teamwork!" said Pritmut sarcastically.

But when her styph flew off, Marva took the lead. Joe was not so lucky. His styph climbed back up and began smashing the side glass again.

"You'll have to open," said Pritmut. "Otherwise, he'll break the glass."

The young man seized the moment, opened the window, and grabbed the beast by the neck with one hand. The monster yelled, trying to twist and bite the racer, but Joe punched him in the nose. The animal twisted and scratched the racer's hand, leaving a deep cut. Holding onto the steering wheel with his other hand, Joe drove around another lava flow and pushed the monster into it with all his strength.

The landscape changed.

"The hurricane valleys of the planet Urak." said Pritmut.

The racer looked ahead. In the distance, huge grey columns rose from the ground, stretching to the sky.

"Tornados?" exclaimed Joe.

"Not just ordinary tornados. They are conscious and absorb everything in their path."

The Lizard raced towards them as large hailstones drummed on its hood. They were so heavy that they left the surface of the car covered in dents.

Huge columns were now rushing straight at him. All sorts of things were spinning in them at great speed, destroying everything they hit.

"Concentrate!" barked Pritmut. "Maneuver 3854, 700, 328, 834 to 309, 624 to 549."

The tornado pulled the Lizard and the car into its grip. The car began creaking as it spun around in a circle.

"It got you!" the coach shouted.

He continued to dictate the settings fast, and Joe, who saw only showers of rain streaming down the windshield, could not make anything out.

"If the second one comes up before you break out, you're screwed!"

Out of the watery mess in front of him grew a second, and then a third tornado. They headed straight at the Lizard, that was trying to escape from the first one.

"Left at 355! I said left! 495 to 487! 984 to 385! 349 to 937!" Joe had never heard Pritmut's voice sound so intense.

But at some point, three tornadoes surrounded the Lizard as if in a huddle. Their funnels began to untwist each other, so that their grip on the Lizard loosened. The car managed to pull forward and Joe shot ahead as fast as he could away from this place.

"That was something," he said.

Pritmut exhaled the spice smoke nervously. Suddenly, Joe winced at the pain in his side. "What happened?" the coach asked.

Joe forced a careless smile.

"Nothing."

"Don't lie to me, kid! This is your wound!" Instead of replying, Joe turned on the music.

"Did you know we had this option all this time, Coach?" he asked, almost dancing.

The Lizard escaped smaller tornados, and little by little, the valley of the hurricanes was left behind.

Just when Joe thought he could breathe easy again, a huge wall of water rose in front of him. It stretched along the entire perimeter of the horizon and rose endlessly upwards, so no top was in sight.

"Aria's underwater world," Pritmut said.

"Noi!"

"Yes, Joe?"

"How is the underwater function?"

"Fully configured. Just don't open the windows." "Haha! Coach, we're ready."

The Lizard at full speed flew into the water wall and the world around it was plunged into silence.

Algae, corals, and underwater plants created a spectacular world with fish and ocean animals scurrying around. Joe felt like a child seeing an aquarium for the first time in his life and couldn't stop gazing at it.

At the Golden Tribune, the guests vigorously discussed the views.

"The Lagrians did their best," said Barver. "Before, the races were not so scenic, but now we seem to be immersed in the worlds of other planets."

"Agreed," answered Zelga. "They know their business. After all, the Play Like Gods corporation has long occupied the main place in the space tourism market."

"I have no idea where they get such technology." Marken tried to catch the hologram fish floating around him.

"Do not forget that with their technology, they can easily take the life of anyone who stands in their way!" reminded Nuan.

"Then why haven't they taken control of Orion already?" objected Barver. "Perhaps Lagra is not as bad as you think."

"Let's not start this dispute again," Zelga said. "The agreements have been signed and we can only watch what is happening. Right, Ulit? Today, you are more silent than ever."

"With the help of Lagra or not, I sent my brother to certain death." "Such is the trait and the destiny of all shifters."

"I'm not a shifter!" Ulit took off his glasses and sat on the sofa. Zelga poured him a drink, and he drank it in one gulp.

In this underwater world, Joe mentally prepared himself for the dangers it will bring. He didn't have to wait long.

"On the left, a flock of shtikhas," said Pritmut.

Joe saw a few sharks with octopus-like tentacles. They rushed towards the car. He drove into a narrow opening, but another car blocked his exit.

"Long time no see, Joe," he heard.

Binnie and Harvey appeared out of nowhere.

Joe shot an energy wave and Binnie's car turned and bounced opening the way. However, the shtikha swam behind Joe's car with its tentacles and dragged the Lizard deeper.

The same thing happened to Harvey's car. They were both dragged down. Of course, Binnie would not leave his brother. He followed them, pushing the shtikha's tentacles. Gradually, its grip loosened, and Harvey broke free.

"Spin around your axis," Pritmut ordered.

Joe did that and got out of the shark's grip, allowing the Lizard to catch up with the brothers.

Joe turned his head to the left and saw that the crack in the window made by the styph was growing.

"Coach, we might be in trouble," he said.

"Move faster and we may be able to escape before the glass breaks," the slug said.

But suddenly, all three cars stopped. In front of them was a huge water monster with many heads and an endless number of arms. It grabbed everything it could reach stuffing it into its many mouths. The creature was occupying the entire space, and it was impossible to bypass it.

Binnie and Harvey flew forward, but the monster immediately reached for them, and they recoiled back. Joe did the same, but he couldn't get past either.

"I'm stuck!"

"Right." Pritmut was thinking. "The car won't go past it."

"So?"

"Swim."

"But I can't see the surface!"

"You'll drive as far as you can, then Noi will take the car."

Joe gathered himself up and at full speed moved straight to the monster. He dodged its grasping hands and reached one of its heads.

"Noi, take the car!" Joe shouted and took a deep breath.

In the next moment, he was in the water without a car.

"Come on, swim faster before it notices you!" said Pritmut into his ears.

Joe got to an opening near its neck and slipped through it, leaving the monster behind. There in the distance, he saw the Lizard on the sea bed, lit by a beam of light. But how could he get inside?

"You must catch one of the air bubbles," said the coach. Nearby, Joe saw bubbles emerging from an underwater crater.

"Hurry up before the mermaids of Muria notice you."

Joe looked around. Thick fish tails flashed nearby every so often. His lungs felt they were going to explode; he couldn't hold on much longer. Hiding behind a thicket of seaweed, he waited until there was no danger around to make a grab for one of the bubbles.

"Now get to the car, quick!" Pritmut commanded.

When Joe reached the bubble, he realized that he could cover his entire car with it. He managed to do that and then got inside and finally gasped for air.

"No time to rest," shouted Pritmut. "Get going!"

Joe was still out of breath, but obeyed Pritmut's command. He noticed that Noi had already fixed the side window. But as soon as he wanted to turn on the motion levers and move, he became stunned at what he saw.

In front of him, humanoid creatures appeared. They did not inspire fear. Just the opposite. Their faces were calm and so beautiful that time seemed to stop for Joe at that moment.

"Don't look them in the eyes, Myers!" the coach barked. "All the engines at full speed! We got to go!"

Joe couldn't help but look them in the eyes. They were endless and bottomless like the starry sky. The mermaids approached the Lizard and touched the windshield.

At that moment, something scared them away and they scattered to the sides.

"Drive, Joe. I'll hold them back!" He heard. Joe came to his senses.

"Helga? I thought we aren't helping each other anymore."

"I thought so, too," said the girl. "But I realized I want you to win more than anything else!"

The car rushed past, followed by the mermaids whose faces were now distorted with anger and ugliness. Their mouths twisted, revealing crooked, rotten teeth, and they made horrendous that were heard even under water.

Joe wanted to help Helga, but she disappeared from his sight. "Onward!" commanded Pritmut. "No time for sentimentality!" The racer continued, glad to leave the water world behind.

"Helga, are you okay?"

"Yes, I'm out of the water now."

That made him feel better.

Soon Joe left the underwater world too.

He looked around and saw tall iron rocks rising up from the ground.

    "Looks like something from district X2," he said.

"And you're right. Iron Valley from planet K815N6, to be more precise."

"And why is it dangerous?"

But no answer was needed. More than a dozen cyborg dragons were moving straight towards the Lizard. Their shells were made of iron, and huge mouths breathed out pillars of fire.

The car spun around, trying to escape, but more and more of them were approaching. Unable to burn it to ashes, they tried to hit the Lizard with their tails and wings. But Joe and Pritmut were faster.

Marken clapped his hands happily. "District X2! These are our guys!"

"It seems all three finalists are stuck there." Nuan was captivated, too.

"Marva and Hunger are in the lead," said Zelga. "Look how they try to push each other into the iron jaws of the dragons."

"Soon they will see Joe, and the real race will begin."

And so it happened. Joe quickly caught up with them, and now three cars were spinning, trying to set one up against the other.

"It's a pity Binnie and Harvey fell behind," said Barver disappointedly. "I made huge bets on them even before the first round started."

Ulit turned in the direction of the pavilion where the sponsors were sitting. Lear Juice was pale as chalk and was discussing something in a whisper with Rod Hunger.

Joe had just dodged the jaws of one dragon when another one caught the Lizard in a clawed paw, and a second grabbed Marva's car. Both racers immediately sent the cars to the workshop and began to fall.

They shouted the names of their cars at the same time. The two cars reappeared and hovered in the air.

Joe fell on the roof and before he managed to stand up, Marva jumped on the back of the Lizard with a furious cry and pushed Joe with all her strength. He slipped but managed to grab the edge of the door. For a moment, she lost her balance, and almost fell, too. But when Joe got back on the roof, they began to fight furiously, trying to push each other off.

However, when an iron dragon rushed towards them, they both took the safest option by jumping into their own cars and continuing the race.

"Hunger is far ahead," said Pritmut with disappointment.

"But Coach, she almost pushed me into the dragons' jaws," Joe tried to justify himself.

"The girl is not a problem for you, but Hunger knows his business."

The landscape changed, and the Lizard landed on the ground. Joe shifted gears and pulled the levers, but he couldn't get back up into the air.

"The flight function seems to have failed."

"No, not failed," said Pritmut. "This part of the race is a no-fly stage. Start your engines and go!"

Joe moved ahead. After all this previous time in the air, it felt weird to him to be on the ground, but he remembered the Gurt races, where he always felt in his element. The Lizard crackled as it moved across the hard ground.

"The forests of Murna," Pritmut stated, as outlandish trees, plants and vines began to grow very fast from beneath the ground.

They appeared in the path of the racer so quickly that he barely had time to avoid them. Joe was nimbly navigating the obstacles when, to his surprise, he saw Wut sitting on the ground under a tree.

"Hi there!" Joe screamed and waved to him.

"Good," said Pritmut, exhaling spice smoke. "His car is in the workshop."

Joe laughed, shaking his curls, when suddenly the ground shook and began to move apart. Pritmut dictated the settings at such a speed that Joe could barely keep up with him. At some point, there seemed to be no more land under the Lizard's wheels. Joe turned the car on its side in order to drive into a narrow opening.

"The bridge!" shouted Pritmut.

Joe rolled out onto the bridge and breathed a sigh of relief. "The bridge is collapsing!" yelled Pritmut even louder.

Joe looked back and immediately sped up. The bridge behind him was disappearing faster than he could go. However, he delighted himself with the skill he used to out-run the collapse.

"Coach Pritmut," Joe pleaded, panting. "Can I stop and rest for just a minute?"

He felt exhausted and dripped with sweat. The pain in his side stabbed him so hard that he couldn't bear it, and the cut on the arm was bleeding.

"No," barked the coach. "Why can't you ever pull yourself together, Myers?"

Joe swallowed his pain and took to the air. The landscape around him had changed, and the Lizard flew faster than a ray of light.

The Golden Tribune was loudly discussing the players, their failures and victories.

"Joe seems to be tired," Zelga stated. "But he is leading, and Hunger is still waiting for his car."

"Attention!" came the voice of the coordinator Tewie. "Now the fun begins." Barver rubbed his hands.

Ulit's heart trembled as he turned to the table of sponsors, from where the coordinator was speaking.

"You all know that the race is organized by our dear sponsors, among which the two most significant are Rod Hunger and Lear Juice."

The two aliens waved their hands to everyone present.

"Under an agreement with the Interstellar Committee, the Play Like Gods corporation provides sponsors with the opportunity to play against racers in any segment of the track. They chose the next one."

Tewie opened a box and handed it to them. Rod and Lear each took out a sticker and stuck it on their wrists.

Everyone turned their faces to the screens.

The Lizard was heading through a fog when two giants appeared in front of him.

"What is this?" Joe asked, seeing only a foot that was about to tread on him.

"Congratulations," Pritmut said coldly. "The sponsors are playing against you.

And he began to dictate settings. The giants tried to catch the Lizard with their huge hands, but Joe and Pritmut were quicker. At some point, one of the giants hit Joe with such force that the Lizard twisted in the air

several times, but Joe handled his car so well it began moving between giants like a fly.

The Hall of the Golden Tribune watched as Rod and Lear twirled and turned, unable to catch Joe.

This struggle exhausted the racer, and everyone saw that he was weakening.

"Is this fair?" Ulit exclaimed.

"Why not?" Barver shrugged his shoulders. "They have sons in the race!"

"The universe is fundamentally unfair," Nuan said thoughtfully.

"But Joe and Pritmut are doing great." Marken tried to cheer him up. Rod and Lear teamed up and blocked Joe's way. One of them leaned over and caught Joe.

But at that moment, Ulit ran up and attacked the sponsors. He knocked Rod down and jumped on Lear's back, screaming.

Joe used this unexpected opportunity to move past the giants so fast that they could no longer catch him.

The whole hall laughed and applauded.

"What does this mean?" raged Rod, tearing the sticker off his wrist. "Only that I evened the odds," Ulit yelled back, adjusting his glasses. But he was already being pulled away from the sponsors' table. Barver frowned, but Zelga, Nuan, and Marken laughed and clapped

their hands.

"This is our hero!"

The Lizard flew forward, leaving the Giants behind. The scenery had changed again, and Joe was flying over a thin pink stream among high mountains.

"Now what?" the racer asked, barely able to hold the wheel. Every muscle in his body ached.

"Archers of the planet Zur," answered Pritmut. "Here, you need all your reaction and speed."

But Joe had almost none left. In the next moment, an arrow pierced straight into the iron covering of the Lizard's hood. In the distance, Joe saw a group of tall, thin creatures with bows. They were all aiming at the Lizard, and before the young man had time to blink, a series of arrows flew straight at him.

Pritmut dictated the settings, but even he could not catch every motion of the shooters appearing from nowhere. They hid behind the trees and ran after the car so fast that Joe could hardly outrun them.

The Lizard streaked through the air with unpredictable movements, but even so, the arrows continued to pierce its surface. One of them broke the side window, and the second rushed through it and almost hit Joe in the head, but he managed to duck in time.

"Just a little more - ten miles," said Pritmut.

But it seemed to Joe that either he or the Lizard was about to collapse.

"Five miles."

The Lizard started a tailspin. With a whistle sound, it headed downwards, almost flying into the stream, and then continued to fly in zigzags.

Suddenly, a sharp pain shot through Joe's shoulder. He screamed as he realized that it was one of the arrows.

"They got me, Coach!"

"Don't slow down, Myers. Only two miles left!"

The Lizard rushed forward and soon the valley was left behind.

"Land on the ground and let Noi fix the glass." Pritmut commanded. Joe took out a first aid kit. He barely got out of the car and fell on the

ground. A dull aching pain pierced his side, his shoulder bled and burned with fire, and the blood was hammering in his temples.

"You must break the arrow and remove it," said the coach. "Then apply a bandage that will stop the bleeding."

The racer's hands were trembling. He almost fainted as he knelt down, screamed, and broke the arrow. The pain intensified.

"I can't," Joe said. "You can, Myers."

Joe grabbed the edge of the arrow. "Pull it out!"

Joe screamed and pulled with all his might. His wound was now bleeding profusely.

"Now apply the bandage."

Everything was swimming before his eyes, but he took out a bandage and applied it to the wound. It automatically found the place where it was needed, tightened itself and stopped the bleeding.

"Now the antidote."

"There is poison in the arrows?" Joe began to hallucinate.

"Take the blue jar in the first aid kit."

The racer took out five jars. They all looked blue to him. "Third from the left," said Pritmut.

Joe drank it and laid on the ground. A terrible chill ran through his body, and he began to shake.

"I can't, coach," he said, laying on the ground. "I give up." Pritmut was silent for a few moments, but then said,

"Do you know why I agreed to help you? Not because of the water or the planet. I saw a winner in you, Joe."

"You say that on purpose." the racer said through his gritted teeth.

"Well," Pritmut exhaled calmly. "You may not know yet, but you will win. It's written in your pupils. I am from the planet Manzur. We have our own specialties. I've read thousands of racers."

"Is it true?"

"Haven't you heard the saying 'Pritmut only picks winners.' Do you know why? Because they bend reality to suit them. They have their own gravity, like stars and planets. And I was born with this unique flair -   to recognize racers like you."

"You're not lying?"

"Why would I? Even before the start, I knew that you would come first," Pritmut said, exhaling his spice smoke again.

Joe slowly got up.

"Then I call Noi."

"Go ahead, son. We don't want to ruin the plans of the universe, do we?"

The Lizard appeared and Joe crawled towards it. The hallucinations were gone, but his head was spinning. The young man climbed into the cabin and buckled up. The pain was unbearable, but he put on his goggles and turned on the engines.

"734 to 156, 923 to 238."

And the Lizard was in the air again.

"What's next?" Joe asked weakly.

"I don't know," said Pritmut. "This is an unpredictable segment of the track. Tell me what you see."

Suddenly Joe screamed as loudly as he could and veered sharply to the left, and then to the right.

"What's there?"

"Seventh star! I think the dead are flying towards me!" "Ah. Tunnel of fears."

In front of Joe were creatures which were difficult to imagine. The mere sight of them sent a wave of freezing cold over his body, and his hands trembled more than from the poison of the arrows. But Joe avoided them all and soon entered a new section.

"Hunger is on your tail, Joe. Be careful," said Pritmut.

Soon clouds of darkness started swirling around. Their pattern was more complex and larger than in the first two races, and the obstacles appeared even more unexpectedly. Wut's blue car flashed behind Joe, and he heard his calm but tense voice.

"How are you, Joe?"

But the racer was silent.

"You're probably already planning how you'll celebrate your victory?" "None of your business, Hunger."

"Why? I'll be happy if you win. But it's no secret that you are planning to run away with Elira Bright."

Joe's hand trembled and he almost flew into the black cloud.

"Beautiful dreams. And I don't want to disappoint you, but just because we are friends, I'll tell you one little secret."

Joe was silent.

"Elira Bright is a robot. It is designed to help racers in their difficult moments. You didn't know this? Hm. My father is a sponsor, and he knows all about it."

"You're lying," Joe forced out despite his pain.

"What did you expect from X2? Her father lost her when she was 10. He built a new version of her out of metal and updates it every year as she gets older. But she's not real. She's just a robot with a program instead of a brain. Hah, you're a complete newbie. Let's be honest. If she were real, she would never choose you."

"Joe!" There was an insistent voice of the coach. "Whatever he tells you, don't listen!"

"I won't, Coach."

Sweat rolled down Joe's face. Everything in front of his eyes was out of focus. He could barely hold the steering wheel.

Wut hit the Lizard with force so that it turned 360 degrees making it fall behind, almost flying into a cloud of darkness.

"584 to 274, 495 to 234, maneuver 2678!" dictated Pritmut.

The cars leveled up again and creaked as they scraped each other's side.

"You must kick him out of the game," said Pritmut insistently. "There is no other way."

But no matter how angry Joe was, he did not want to push Wut into a cloud of darkness.

The cars were hitting and damaging each other, until at some point, Wut overtook Joe again. However, he immediately ran into an obstacle and his car braked sharply. The Lizard slammed into it and its hood shrank.

Joe barely kept control, but Hunger's car rolled over him. They both were falling into a cloud of darkness, but at the last moment Joe pushed them both away from it. Wut's car fell to the ground. The Lizard made a cracking sound and followed. Then there was a blow and pain that was unbearable.

Joe lay unconscious when the coach's insistent shouting brought him back to his senses.

"Get up, Myers! There are two more racers behind you."

There was no Lizard nearby. On the left, Joe saw unconscious Wut and his completely destroyed car. Above them, there was a cloud of darkness.

"Noi can't fix the Lizard, Joe. It will take too long," came Noi's shaking voice. "The brakes have completely failed."

"Is it only the brakes that failed?" Joe could barely focus. "So, I can keep going?"

The Lizard reappeared before him.

"Get up, Joe! We'll aim for second place!" commanded Pritmut. "No." The racer climbed into the car. "We'll go for first."

"This is impossible, Myers, the brakes have failed!"

"I know."

Joe put on his racing goggles and turned on the screens. The Lizard rose into the air.

"Myers, don't speed up. You just need to cross the first barrier before Marva Tanto does!"

But Joe was rushing forward at full speed. "What are you doing, Myers?" barked Pritmut.

"You yourself said that I am a winner," Joe answered. "I have it written on my pupils."

"Joe, this is all nonsense! Everything I said, I made up to support you!"

"You did well, Coach."

The Lizard circled the clouds of darkness.

"Look, Joe, second place is what you need! Take your winnings and go with the Bright girl to some perfect planet!"

"Wut said she is just a robot," Joe replied, speeding up.

"That's also nonsense, Joe, I was at her parents' wedding. Release the movement levers now!"

"Yeah."

"I'm telling you the truth, Joe!"

"It doesn't matter, Coach. We all know that I'm here for first place."

He drove into a white shining wall of light, and a wall of darkness grew in front of him.

"You've crossed the first barrier," Coach said in confusion.

Right behind him, Joe could see Marva Tanto, so he sped up even more.

"Letting go of the levers now is your last chance!"

"Thank you, Coach. Really, thanks for choosing me," Joe said, almost losing consciousness.

At that moment, it seemed to him that there was someone in the car. Joe turned his head. It was his father. He shook his head and said,

"Being second isn't so bad, Joe. Doing what's best for you, rather than others, is not so bad either."

"No," the racer answered. "I must...must come first!" The father smiled and tapped him on the shoulder. "Then don't be afraid. Just fly to the stars."

He disappeared. Joe switched to Noi's channel.

"Noi, I'm heading straight into the darkness."

"Noi knows," the alien sobbed.

"From my winnings, pay Ike my debts. Give him a million times more."

"Of course, Joe. Anything you ask."

"And Noi, before I'm gone. I have one more question for you. Why did you end up stuck on Melgera? With abilities like yours, it's strange."

"I'll tell you when you come back."

"We both know I'm not coming back, Noi."

The mechanic was silent for a few moments and then said,

"You are, Joe, because you are a shifter. Some use this word today as something fancy. But Noi lived more than a thousand years, and he knows what is coming to Orion. He knew it from the very first moment he saw Joe. You are a shifter, and shifters always find their way."

The sound cut off.

"Noi," Joe called.

But he was not there.

"Coach?"

Again silence.

At an incredible speed, Joe passed the second barrier and rushed forward, unable to stop the car.

"Where there is no horizon and the bottom is not seen, the Seventh Star shines, clear and bright, like a dream." He was singing, "Why is the star the Seventh? Who can count the stars?" was his last thought as he plunged into an endless darkness.

Ulit looked at the screens for a long time, not believing what he was seeing.

"Racer Joe Dee Myers from the planet Melgera on the periphery of Orion broke all records by coming first in the 757th Interstellar Mega Race. In addition, he is the first lucky one in history to succeed! His victory has guaranteed all the benefits of Orion for his planet. But the sad thing is that he drove into the wall of darkness, and we won't be able to see him again!" the announcer said.

The entire Hall of the Golden Tribune applauded, turning to Ulit. They came up and shook his hands. Some looked into his eyes sympathetically, others with a cold gaze. And he just stood there, dazed.

"Following Myers, Marva Tanto arrived second, after her, Mardo Keaton, Helga Lutto, the Juice Brothers and..."

"Congratulations." Marken patted Ulit on the shoulder. "We all pretty much knew which of you two was the shifter."

"But it's not me."

Ulit took off his glasses and touched his face with his hands. Barver got closer to him and whispered,

"Shifters will do everything for their goals. Even sacrifice their own brother."

"Be that as it may, you have been offered a new position: Head of the Committee for Work with Planets on the Periphery. What do you think?" asked Zelga. "We need people like you!"

But Ulit still could not believe that he had lost his brother.

"I didn't even say goodbye to him properly."

"Joe! Joe! Joe! Deeee! Deeee! Deeee! Myyyyyyyers!" chanted the crowds all over the universe and again, and again, "Joe! Joe! Joe! Dee! Dee! Dee! Myyyyyyers!"

Ulit stood and continued to look at the screens in confusion, unable to move. Before that, he had never imagined his life without his brother. And now that that moment had arrived, everything else seemed so unimportant.

He shuddered when Rod Hunger and Lear Juice approached him.

"Can't decide whether to celebrate or cry?" asked Rod. "Do you think you and your brother did such a good, noble deed? Do you even know how many planets on the periphery will now demand access to Orion?"

"There will be a war," drawled Lear. "A huge universal war, and we all know whose fault it will be."

When they left, Ulit felt that all his thoughts and emotions turned into chaos. He didn't think about it. He believed in his brother's victory from the very beginning. But now, when this victory became a reality, it was as if he found himself in a new world with different new rules, and there, without Joe, he was so helpless.

Ulit turned away from the screens and ran into a portal. He was transported to the town of racers, where the celebration was in full swing. Joe's pictures and videos were everywhere, and the crowds were chanting his name.

"Ulit Dee Myers," he heard behind him.

He turned. Elira Bright stood there. She smiled softly. "You will be late for the awards ceremony."

"I ... I won't go," said Ulit.

"It's a pity," said Elira. "He fought so well, your brother. The winnings will be transferred to your account. Take this."

She handed him the champion's medal. Ulit took it. Suddenly, Elira's eyes became glassy, her eyelashes fluttered uncontrollably, and her head made an unnatural turn. But it stopped. The girl smiled again.

"You'll be late for the awards ceremony," she repeated.

"I won't go," repeated Ulit.

"It's a pity. He fought so well, your brother. The winnings will be transferred to your account. Take this."

She extended her empty hand to him, but then realized that he already had the medal, smiled, turned around, and left.

Ulit looked at her leaving, then at the medal. Drones hovered around him. He moved away, trying to hide from them.

Helga then appeared in front of him. She pointed to the entrance to a small cafe.

"Helga? Helga Lutto?"

The girl nodded. They sat down at the table.

"I'm so sorry. I'm so sorry," she said.

"Thank you for helping him there underwater." "It doesn't matter now."

"Indeed," agreed Ulit. "Now everything seems to have lost its meaning."

But the girl shook her head.

"No. I read a lot about Lagra and about darkness. No one knows exactly what happens to those who fall into it. There is no evidence that they are dying!"

Ulit sighed.

"None ever come back."

"We'll find out! We can't lose hope! I will do anything to bring Joe back!"

But at that moment, the crowd filled the cafe. They shouted and surrounded Ulit, asked questions and took photographs.

Helga stood up and disappeared into the crowd. Ulit looked at her leaving. She was like a bright light in the loneliness of the universe. But it was enough to give him the strength to move on.

*** Go, Joe! by Zinaida Kirko***

TheHappyStoryGarden.com

<u>*Other books by Zinaida Kirko:*</u>

Three Incredible Adventure Stories
Dream World
Dragon Island
W712
Jackie's Adventures in the World of Letters.